DETROIT PUBLIC LIBRARY

3 5674 00580307 8

W9-BXM-693

DETROIT PUBLIC LIBRARY

BL

DATE DUE

SEASONS
AND
MOMENTS

JOHN HAASE

SIMON AND SCHUSTER • NEW YORK

C. 1

ALL RIGHTS RESERVED
INCLUDING THE RIGHT OF REPRODUCTION
IN WHOLE OR IN PART IN ANY FORM
COPYRIGHT © 1971 BY JOHN HAASE
PUBLISHED BY SIMON AND SCHUSTER
ROCKEFELLER CENTER, 630 FIFTH AVENUE
NEW YORK, NEW YORK 10020

FIRST PRINTING

SBN 671-20971-X
LIBRARY OF CONGRESS CATALOG CARD NUMBER: 78-156149
DESIGNED BY EVE METZ
MANUFACTURED IN THE UNITED STATES OF AMERICA

NOV 16 '71

BL

For Janice

A successful, fortyish California architect, bored with life and marriage, journeys to Copenhagen and the French Riviera with an attractive young set designer.

1

CASSY HAD FOUND Loco Joe's in the Portola district of San Francisco. It was a shabby, dark establishment frequented by working people who were residents of that neighborhood. It would be like Cassy to find a place like Loco Joe's, and I could not only see her methodically cruising the area in her station wagon, the doors carefully locked, a pair of brown leather gloves on the seat next to her, I could even understand her choosing this dismal boîte. We would be safe. We were more immune from discovery here, only three miles from Pacific Heights, than in the lobby of the Plaza in New York, or at the foot of the Spanish Steps in Rome.

I looked at the soiled mirror behind the teak back bar and checked the knot on my tie for the tenth time, trying to see between the racks of Polish sausage and the illuminated beer advertisements showing a running stream, which proved to be only diuretic. My countenance somewhat amused me, dressed as I was in a latter-day Ivy League Brooks Brothers flannel suit, my fingernails prudently trimmed and polished, my shoes carefully shined, my shirts chastely monogrammed on my left sleeve.

Even Mary had commented this morning, which was rare.

"That tie looks nice with that suit."

"Oh, I hadn't noticed."

"Should do things for you in Chicago."

"Chicago, yes."

Cassy was late and the bartender asked whether I wanted another drink. I nodded, not really caring about drinking this early in the day but feeling obliged to pay the price of admission.

I watched the front door, waiting for Cassy, always a trifle late, composed, opening statement prepared, trim, beautiful. Two streetcar conductors sat next to me, their dark-blue uniforms shiny and coarse. They ordered two bourbons, gulped them down, paid and departed.

Cassy and I had met at Loco Joe's fifteen times now. She was the statistician in our union and all the meetings were short, nervous and served no other purpose than to affirm a few minutes which were ours, a secret we could share like embezzlement or syphillis.

I had known Cassy for almost sixteen years now and she had known Mary for longer than that. I suppose they had mutually discovered the function of a bidét when they were six or perhaps ridden to the hounds when they were four; I never knew the reason for their bond other than their proximal social life. We saw each other constantly, moving as we did in the same circle of friends, actually finding more access and privacy in large gatherings than these silly rendezvous. But why had it taken this long to reach this point?

Certainly no self-respecting philanderer would call Cassy and my relationship "an affair." An affair after all meant a consummation, two people sharing each other's bodies and guilts, certainly those in equal proportion. But in our situation there had really not been any pleasure, only guilt, and I strongly wondered now how much I truly loved Cassy to let all this prevail for so many years, taking each rebuff philosophically, sensing no urgency to replace the voids with passions.

"An independent spirit"; that was probably the favorite description of Cassy in our group. It was really just another label for people who had a need to label each other. Of course it was presumed that everyone was terribly nice, well-meaning, honest and upstanding. We did not steal each other's wallets; we treated help fairly, threw up in our own master bathrooms and managed to cover our beds with Supercale sheets twice a week.

There were women who were labeled moody or fun loving; others were praised for their superior motherhood, their facility in the kitchen, their ability to throw large parties; there were artists and misers, and teases; but two San Franciscans could meet at the Excelsior in Cairo, have a gin and tonic, mention Cassy Donahue and beat each other to the draw saying, "a very independent spirit."

Cassy and I had traced the genesis of this label one night and concluded that all of it stemmed from a few minor events during her thirty-six uneventful years. She had refused to be a debutante, she had studied geology at Stanford, which was considered a masculine major, she had four children by natural childbirth and posed once in the nude for a local sculptor, which, with its sexual overtones added as the fixative, added substance to all the other rather commonplace rebellions.

But these were only the early years with Cassy. Of course I had kissed her and had held her at a New Year's Eve party. I had seen her partially undressed when we had adjoining summer houses on the Peninsula. I had seen her in her bathing suit, catching a glimpse of her breast as she gathered the wet towels at the end of a strenuous summer day about the pool; I could even remember a trip to the liquor store one evening. It was a warm, windless night and we had needed wine. I volunteered to drive to Palo Alto and Cassy had said, "Wait, Peter, I'll come with you," and I in my headiness had taken that spontaneity as an offer, perhaps.

"Let's go to a motel," I said. "Let's find a room. Come on."

"No," Cassy said. "No, we'd better get back. It's too risky. I'd look so flushed, Al would know the moment I came into the room."

I had not pressed the point that night, and there had been other opportunities, equally precarious, equally viable which I had also not pursued, and so our affair, if it had any structure at all, could be said to have been built with the clay of innumerable small desires all carefully wrapped in foil, restricted by a strong sense of guilt, totally resistant to heat and passion.

Of course I was also to blame for this state of affairs. I admired Cassy. I loved her looks. She had a certain freshness, an athletic grace; she seemed just slightly less monotonous that the other women in our crowd, and still I was quite willing to coast along all these years with a prolonged look, a knee touching under the table, a few intimate words at the symphony during intermission. I found it all almost amusing and would have been the first to agree with Cassy had she said that it was all nonsense and we should cease and desist.

But Cassy prevailed, and though I have no great feeling of conquest because of her attraction for me, I know that somehow I was shepherding her through her thirties. She had been a beautiful girl, socially prominent, athletic, elegant, used to much attention, much excitement; the role of mother, of wife, the role of subjugation toward her own daughter, equally lovely, was no doubt difficult. In some bizarre way, I was filling that void.

It had been Cassy who suggested these trysts, and when after a number of nervous meetings I found her only prevailing emotion to be fear, I suggested we call a halt; but perhaps feeling that if she were to let go of me it would be like letting go of youth itself, Cassy suggested, probably more in haste than in prudence, that we should try to spend one weekend together. A few days we could call our own. Mornings and middays, evenings and nights, and I had agreed, not because I am so charitable, but I, too, wanted either to light the fire or put it out. We had been banking it for so many years.

Sitting here in this alien bar I could not help wondering what it would be like to share a bed with Cassy. No matter how well I knew her, I realized that the act of love would make her reveal something of herself which I had never known. I did not expect her to be an overtly sensuous woman; I rather suspected that she would be frightened, modest, somewhat ritualistic after a good many years of monogamy. Still somehow tonight Cassy would be fulfilling a bargain, but tomorrow, in the leisure of an empty day she would soften, knowing perhaps that I too was frightened, that I wanted nothing overt or totally selfish. Perhaps tomorrow, I thought, we could begin to make love.

～～∽～～

MY COURTSHIP with Mary had really not been overly long, although my two-year absence serving in the Navy coupled with the time it took to finish my studies in architecture made the period of our engagement seem quite lengthy, and I watched (which is the proper word to use) the machinery of marriage go into full gear once the day of my graduation became known.

I can still remember frantic months of preparation for Mary and her mother. There seemed to be endless shopping, endless lists, immense problems of selection and protocol, all of it underscored by a rather sedate growling by old man Danner who never mustered the courage to tell his own womenfolk how much all of it was costing but nevertheless managed to fill me with a certain sense of guilt and responsibility for all the forthcoming activities.

I had really not wanted such a large wedding, cared little whether the reception was at the Fairmont or the Mark Hopkins or the Fleishacker Zoo, tried but failed to help select patterns of china, crystal or silver and somehow resented the number of personal friends or family I was allowed to supply for the event. Week by week I found myself growing more and more outside of the preparatory team, watching Mary grow paler and more intense, still somehow loving all the trappings, the endless array of proper things which must be attended to in this a socially prominent union.

Sexually our courtship had been sparse, partially because I had been relatively young myself. Young, unconfident, intimidated and certainly for good measure, because Mary had prevailed and prevented our taking any risks which might only cause great pain to everyone later. I could only remember two distinct occasions when I had seriously tried to take Mary to bed before our marriage: once before I was shipped overseas, and once after the war when Mary had come to Phoenix for a weekend to visit me at school.

She was convincing the first time and I could sympathize with her position of not wanting to worry for a month whether I had left her with child while I faced possible death in the Atlantic, but I was less sympathetic in Phoenix. She had come alone, rented a perfectly good hotel room; it had been a long warm, Saturday night. "My parents," Mary had said, "let me come because they knew they could trust me, Peter. I'm not about to let them down."

After the vows had been said and the carefully sculptured wedding bouquet from Poderata and Baldochi had been caught by a young niece stationed at the foot of the circular stairway, after I had changed from tails to tweeds and Mary from satin to a chaste linen suit, after we had departed in Mary's brand-new Plymouth heading for Lake Tahoe, I

13

was more numb than anxious, more weary than curious; and when finally after a tortuous five-hour drive we settled in our bridal chamber of the Tahoe Tavern and brushed the rice from the folds of the luggage we looked more like two people rendezvousing after a serious complicated robbery than two lovers about to begin marriage.

Mary had carried modesty to extremes in the beginning years, and those first nights of our honeymoon seemed to be spent in total darkness, dressing and undressing in separate rooms, necking in bed, and then only briefly, not talking, not exploring, barely fulfilling our roles of newlyweds.

Our honeymoon had lasted two weeks, and I returned to San Francisco quite depressed.

I could not guess the sexuality of Mary. We had never really discussed the subject seriously. Somehow I had envisioned long hours in bed. I had hoped for fun, for playfulness, for intimacy, the relief of not fearing conception; for communal showers, dressing and undressing; all natural fantasies, I suppose, all of them methodically shattered by Mary. She displayed neither curiosity nor lust, minimally fulfilling her conjugal obligations, but more anxious to return to the rounds of parties awaiting us, more shopping, more selections, more organizing.

～∞～

IT WAS five-twenty now and I was watching the door anxiously and feeling uncomfortable because I knew I was being watched by others around the bar. I *was* anxious now. My things were neatly packed and stored in the trunk of a rented car across the street. The reservations were made, the timetable had been carefully planned, the moves were all meticulous.

We had always met on Fridays. Cassy's husband spent that evening at the club and I felt no qualms about finally phoning her home. I dialed the number thinking if one of the children answered I would replace the receiver without identifying myself, knowing then that she was on her way, but Cassy answered.

"Peter."

"Yes."

"I was waiting for your call."

"What's the matter?"

"Toby's sick."

"What's the matter with him?"

"Just a cold."

"Well?"

"I'm afraid."

"Of what? Have you called a doctor?"

"It's not that serious."

"Then I don't understand."

"Maybe it's an omen."

"Oh come on, since when have you gone in for astrology?"

"Peter?"

"What?"

"Peter, don't be angry . . . what if Toby gets worse, and I'm not here?"

"For Christ's sake, Cass, you've got a housekeeper. Al will be home."

"You're right. I know you're right. Everything's packed. I'm all ready. I just don't feel right."

"Look Cass, forget it. Forget the whole thing."

"Peter, please."

"What do you want? I'm supposed to be in Chicago over the weekend. What do you want me to do? Go to the "Y" and bury myself?"

"Don't be angry. What do you want me to be? What shall I do?"

"I don't care Cassy. I'll have one more drink and then I'll leave. Do what you want."

I hung up the telephone and I stood next to the wall phone for a minute seeing Cassy in her bedroom, no doubt seated on the well-made monogrammed bedspread, its edges neatly squaring off the single bed next to her husband's. She had spoken quietly, probably straightening a small photograph on the night stand or dusting the rim of a diminutive gold alarm clock with her left hand, and I could see her now, standing, tugging the same bedspread to remove the evidence of having sat on it. I noticed patrons of the bar watching me, not me in particular since I was not such a striking personage, but the cut of my suit, perhaps the good silk of my necktie, the chaste small gold cuff links which fastened my shirt to my wrists, all evidence of some affluence. And though I know I made too much of this as I returned to my seat at the bar, I found it necessary to quote some football statistic to the bartender, to comment on the rawness of the weather, but I was not to be rewarded with easy camaraderie and soon found myself staring into the meniscus of my martini and knew that that colorless liquid would have no answers to my predicament.

Toby's cold was a sham. Of course the boy might have the sniffles, but that is an endemic state of affairs in a family of four children. She was afraid of being discovered and this I could understand, but it was the audacity to call it off at the last minute, the bald-faced temerity to let me sit here in this stupid bar knowing full well that I had made careful preparations for weeks, that once she had suggested the weekend, I had planned with such prudence so that no one should get hurt.

I considered leaving, whether she came or not, but I knew that this would only play into her hands. She would panic momentarily and then state that I simply was not there when she did arrive, but even that logic was weak. One does not build weeks of expectations, hours of anticipation, only to have them dashed because of some nonsense. I no longer really knew whether I wanted Cassy or consummation. All my efforts demanded some reward. The last thing I needed was a bitch-woman. I had suffered with that long enough.

2

WE HAD CALLED it the Tahoe Rebellion and thinking back
now, it all seems so trivial. For generations, old-line San
Francisco families summered at Lake Tahoe. Some had
homes, others rented cottages, series of rooms at the Tavern,
at Edgebrook, at Fallen Leaf.

This year, eight families, ourselves included, decided to
forego Lake Tahoe in favor of summering on the Peninsula.
We traded the rustic mountain homes for gracious country
houses, we swam in private pools rather than in the icy lakes,
spent evenings discovering new little restaurants, attended
summer stock or sat about each others' patios drinking and
discussing an endless number of irrelevant subjects. The
children were still young, all of our children, there was ade-
quate help to stop their getting in our way, there were endless trouble-free boring hours to recoup the strength none of
us had really lost during the labors of the previous year.

·

It was one such evening at L'omelette, a chic small restaurant near Atherton where Cassy perhaps verbalized more explicitly all the frustrations common to her and to almost all the rest of us. We had been drinking around our pool and Cassy and I, still sitting at the bar, continued to drink that evening. It had been a pleasant conversation, I remembered, warm, easy, and we had reached some accord. Looking back on it now, there was nothing really unusual about it; we were old friends, ten years into monogomy. The confessions were routine, the revelations commonplace, but all of them coming from Cassy; her utter candor, her feelings of hopelessness, the boredom with the sexual part of her marriage, the lack of romance, of surprise, gave me perhaps a ray of hope, a light in the tunnel.

"I've had so many colds," she said, "so many headaches, backaches, my period seems to last two weeks and is getting more irregular. Goddamn it, Peter, what is wrong?"

I shook my head.

"Look at my husband. Look at all the husbands in our crowd. Up at eight. Downtown at nine-thirty. Home at five. In bed by ten. Day in. Day out. Two evenings out in restaurants, one dinner party, one symphony, ballet, three sessions of intercourse and six white shirts annually bought at Macy's during the sale."

"I don't buy my shirts at Macy's," I protested. "I detest dinner parties."

"You go."

"I go. And if that's all you think about me, to hell with it."

"I'm not talking about you."

"Why not? I'm up at eight. Downtown at nine-thirty."

"You're not a broker, a merchant. You're Peter Trowbridge. A very creative man."

"Home at five. To bed at ten."

"A very successful architect."

"I think you hit the nail pretty much on the head, Cassy."

"There's *got* to be more."

"There can be more."

"It's not only me, Peter. Every girl in our crowd is complaining about the same thing."

"Maybe you're running around with the wrong group of girls?"

"You know them."

"I do. Maybe I'll change my question to a statement."

"I know that a certain boredom has to set in," Cassy said almost defensively.

"Does it?"

"I can't believe you can go to bed with the same person for ten years and still get terribly excited."

"Why not?"

"Because it's always the same person, the same ritual, the same variations on a theme."

I said nothing.

"Well?"

"You're making me say things you may not want to hear."

"Such as?"

"Going to bed with the same person all the time does not *have* to be the same person all the time, the same ritual, whatever."

"Is that what you and Mary have?"

"No."

"That wasn't any of my business. Then how do you know?"

"I don't know, Cassy. I don't know really. I know only that not everyone in this world runs around unhappy. Not everybody believes their lies the way we all do . . . try going to bed with someone you love."

"For ten years?"

"To hell with ten years."

"I think we'd better join the others at the table."

Again I laughed. "What a marvelous title for a book."

"What?"

" 'I think we'd better join the others at the table.' "

I noticed a coolness between Cassy and myself after this conversation, as if perhaps she regretted speaking so frankly to me, but this distance slowly diminished and once more we found ourselves sequestered from the crowd, sharing a spot on the stern of my sailboat, a corner of a loge during an opera, and more and more we felt the nervous presence of our friends, our spouses until one evening Cassy said, "Christ, Peter, I wish there was someplace we could sit and talk without everyone forever staring at us, saying, 'well, there goes Cassy and Peter . . .' "

From this remark had stemmed our trysts. It is a ludicrous word, and certainly did not describe our meetings. Far from being illicit or intimate, far from being suggestive or promising, I found Cassy only hemmed in by tradition, constantly in fear someone would discover us. Our discussions were neither suggestive nor gay like those of lovers but only constant atonements, for what I don't know. We had, it's true, a few hours to ourselves, but we made no use of them at all.

I put down my drink and saw Cassy enter the bar. I had already settled with the bartender and rose, took her arm and followed her to her car.

She wore a navy-blue suit, a white blouse, white gloves, no hat, no jewelry; a small purse lay on the seat beside her and I could see a small overnight bag on the floor of the back seat. She looked so obviously guilty, so transparent and foolishly inept that all I could do was laugh.

"You're a fallen woman," I said, and I don't really know why I had expressed what I felt.

"You can make all the fun of me you want Peter, but where am I going to park this damned car? Did you ever think of that?"

"Yes, I did."

"Well, don't you think we should?"

Cassy had continued driving and we were going in the opposite direction of my rented automobile.

"The first thing I would suggest is that you stop going in this direction."

Cassy obeyed and pulled over to the curb, then I reached over and kissed her cheek.

"Can't that wait? I'm really nervous."

"Just pull over and let me drive."

I drove the car to a public garage and while Cassy waited at the office I explained to the owner that I would like to park the vehicle for two days, ascertained that he would be open on our return and paid him in advance. Then I rejoined her.

"What did you say to him?"

"I asked him to park the car for a couple of days. That's his business."

"He saw me take my suitcase out of the car. Didn't he think that was funny?"

"Cassy, I didn't ask him what he thought. . . . Come on, let's get to my car."

We walked the two blocks in silence to my car. I put Cassy's suitcase next to mine in the trunk and opened the door for her. She hesitated for a minute.

"You want to change your mind again?"

"No," she said, "just go, let's go . . . I feel like getting into the trunk with the luggage."

I headed for the Bay Bridge, avoiding much of the traffic of the weekend exodus by taking a number of side streets until I finally reached the bridge approach. The city was now fully clothed in fog, only the tops of a few apartment houses of Telegraph and Russian Hill reached out of the blanket and they looked strangely suspended as if on gauze. I crossed the bridge and we said nothing, and not until the toll-gate operator took my quarter did I say, "You know, he looked suspiciously at us . . ."

"I'm sorry Peter," Cassy said, "I don't blame you for being angry."

"I *was* angry, Cassy, let's forget it. You came, that's all that's important. How's Toby?"

"He'll be all right."

"Good."

"Are you always this resilient, Peter?"

"Yup, ole resilient Pete."

"No, I think that's very admirable."

"Now we're getting somewhere. Do you think you could admire me enough to give me a hello kiss?"

We had left the bridge and I took the Freeway going to Santa Rosa.

"Where are we going, Peter?" Cassy asked, dismissing my request.

"Wouldn't you like a little element of surprise?"

"Don't torture me, Peter, please. Why don't you kill me off once and for all, I'm very very upset . . ."

I made a rather sharp turn to the right and pulled off the road and stopped the car.

"What's wrong, Peter?"

"Everything."

"What do you mean?"

"Cassy," I took hold of her shoulders and she drew back instinctively, "now just be reasonable for a minute."

"I'm trying, Peter . . ."

"No you're not . . . just tell me, did you or did you not suggest we have this weekend?"

"Yes."

"All right." I paused almost in relief. "All right. I just wanted to get this clear."

"I'm sorry Peter."

"I know how you feel, believe me. I don't feel so red-hot myself."

"I'm just so afraid someone will see us . . . I keep staring at every car that passes us."

"Well can you see the faces of anyone in those cars?"

"No. No. I know I'm just being stupid."

"Would you like to turn around Cassy? I am not asking you angrily . . ."

"You would turn around wouldn't you Peter?"

"Why do you ask such a foolish question?"

"Let's keep going."

"Would you like a drink?"

"No, just keep going."

I started the car and drove on.

"You still haven't told me where we're going."

"Wolf Ranch," I said.

"Isn't that the hotel you designed?"

"It is the one . . ."

"Doesn't everybody know you there?"

"No one knows me there. The people I built it for sold it years ago . . . I haven't been there in five years. The new owners don't know me from Adam."

"You mean you gave them your right name?"

"Of course."

"And what name did you give for me?"

"I told them I was coming with my wife."

I watched Cassy pull her skirt over her knees and turn on the radio.

3

I DROVE and we listened to an endless number of meaningless songs interspersed with even more intruding newscasts. Somehow I felt the world should remain suspended until this weekend with Cassy ended; it disturbed me to think that life was going on despite us. I tried not to think of Mary or the children, and Cassy's silence was becoming painful. Perhaps I had overestimated her interest in my architecture and should have found a hotel closer to San Francisco, but I had made the plans and now I was committed. I wished Cassy would make it easier.

"Peter?"

"Yes."

"What did you tell Mary?"

"I told her I had to go to Chicago on business. What did you say?"

"I'm visiting my sister in Phoenix."

"What if Al decides to call you there?"

"I told her what I was doing. She's prepared for that. I'm going to call her later tonight."

"Did you tell her what you were really doing? That you were with me?"

"Yes."

"Didn't that embarrass you?"

"No. My sister and I are very close. She just wondered why I had waited all this time."

It was past seven as I entered Sonoma, a sleepy pleasant little town tucked into the fertile wine country of northern California. Once the state capital under General Vallejo, it had tenaciously clung to its vine-covered charm. I took Cassy to the Country Inn which served a solid, decent Italian dinner. We entered the hotel and I led her to the dining room.

It was an old room, with white-washed brick walls which had almost regained their original earthen-red color, the tables were covered with red-and-white checkered table-clothes, the ceiling groaned from the endless array of flax-covered wine bottles hung on the rafters. Deep-set windows overlooked an old-fashioned garden, its flower beds and fountains illuminated by electric imitation candles. An elderly waitress, spotless in a black satin skirt and white blouse, seated us in a little nook on the side of the main entrance and inquired what we would like to drink and whether we were having dinner. I ordered a bottle of Green Hungarian, a white wine grown locally, and poured, perhaps a little anxiously, into two well-shaped, chilled goblets which the waitress had set on the table. I raised my glass in a toast and Cassy followed.

"How about it?" I asked. "Here's to us?"

"I'll drink to that, Peter." Cassy picked up her glass and almost drained it.

"That's no way to drink that wine."

"I know it Peter. I just want to steady the nerves. You don't know how many times I almost called you this week."

"Look Cassy. We've got a couple of days. Let's enjoy them."

"I know you're right Peter. I just think about that junk I read at the hairdresser. 'Does your husband's friend trouble you?' "

"If it makes you feel any better, your husband isn't my friend."

"Who is?"

"People you wouldn't know."

"Why not?"

"Architects, artists. Draftsmen. Ecologists."

"Why wouldn't I like them?"

"You probably would."

"Then why don't you ever entertain them?"

"You know Mary. Unless you're fifth-generation San Franciscan you don't even exist."

"You sound quite bitter."

"Not bitter, Cassy. Bored. Don't you ever get tired of playing bridge with the same bunch? Aren't you sick of walking down Post Street and running into the same women coming out of Magnin's and Gump's? Aren't you sick of the endless endless parties . . . the utter goddamn predictability of it all."

"No, I can't say that. I really like our life. Most of it

anyway. I like our friends, our home, San Francisco, good or bad . . . I don't know, I've been to New York, Paris, I've spent three months in Zurich getting the boys settled in school. I suppose the best answer I can give is that I feel 'safe' in San Francisco. On top of it, maybe that's it. I know what to wear, and how long I can wait to reciprocate for a dinner party and what to bring as a present for a weekend down in the country."

I listened to Cassy and read a poster tacked on the wall behind her chair.

ANNUAL BARN DANCE
RIO-NIDO
The Hub of the Russian River
Fire Dept. Band. $1.00 Donation!

I had been fourteen, a counselor at Scout Camp, Camp Royaneh, the River, that's what we called it. The Russian River. Rio-Nido, Greensville, Jenner-By-The-Sea, paper lanterns, the first taste of beer, warm summer nights, the sweet smell of Ivory Soap on the neck of a little blond girl, what was her name? She used to call me "teeth" because they had just been straightened and were very even. We'd leave the dance about ten o'clock and sit in one of the rental rowboats discovering the first ecstasies of sex, all talk and fumbling, a bra strap, a stuck zipper, will you call me in the city? Will you take me to the Junior Prom? My mom is making me a formal . . . little girl, little girl, how did that song go. . . .

"You don't feel safe now," I said, "not on top of it?"

29

"No and yes . . ." Cassy said. "I just told you I was in Zurich for three months. I was alone, save for the boys, and they had entered school. I only saw them weekends. I'm not a bad-looking woman. I had a few opportunities to, what is the word? Dally? Experiment?"

"Why didn't you?"

"I was afraid. Of the men. I didn't know them. They were foreign, literally and figuratively."

"And you feel safe with me. Predictable."

"That's not a very nice thing for me to say, Peter. Safe . . . I don't know. I *do* know that you're a nice man. I know what you eat for breakfast and that you change your underwear every day . . . I know you love your children. Those things are all important to me . . . I could ask you the same question. Why aren't you here with some little stewardess or in Las Vegas with a show girl? That's where a lot of the boys go."

"I am here, because I am fond of you . . . no other reason. I've been wanting you alone for years."

"I think, Peter Trowbridge, I've just been told off."

"Cassy, you and I have reached the first point of agreement so far."

"If you will let me phone my sister and powder my nose I may think of something nice to say to you."

The waitress came and placed a relish tray and a plate of antipasto on the table and I ordered dinner in Cassy's absence. I ate some peppers, *garbanzo* beans, a few slices of Italian salami and realized that I was quite hungry. A large Italian family occupied the table next to ours, celebrating something. One could see the familial traits filtering through three generations, each slimmer and fairer than the next. It made me uncomfortable watching the children and I was tempted to have our table changed, but Cassy returned, her short auburn hair combed perfectly. She had removed her suit jacket and even her chaste blouse, perhaps a whiff of very sedate cologne, proved quite aphrodisiacal.

"Feel better?"

"A little. My sister sends her love. You've met her."

The waitress brought the soup, then the pasta, and we finished dinner and another bottle of wine chatting pleasantly like two passengers on a long plane ride, impersonal, forced, somewhat overpowered by external forces.

It was nine o'clock when we returned to the car to continue the journey. We traveled a winding two-lane highway along the Russian River, the darkness pierced occasionally by grim neons advertising roadhouses, tourist cabins, motels, groceries, lumberyards, supermarkets. Kids, sixteen, seventeen still strolled hand in hand along the highway or clustered about open convertibles, the girls trim and naked in their tight little Capris, their shorts, the boys crew-cut and inept.

"Did you ever spend any time on the River when you were a kid Cassy?"

"No. We always went to Tahoe. . . . My family thought the River was too wild."

"It wasn't really, you know. I spent three summers up here. There used to be a trailer camp up here"—I pointed to a grove near the highway—"By God, it's still there. Hundreds of trailers, people from Arkansas, Idaho, Oklahoma, older people, good people, used to have a roaring campfire every night and make popcorn for the kids . . . someone always had a guitar, there'd be singing around that fire . . . even the poor people have fun sometimes."

"You've always played that 'outsider' role, you know it Peter?"

"Outsider?"

"Sure. You've been fighting our group for years."

"Does it show that much?"

"It does to me. It's a losing battle you know . . . people can't help being rich any more than they can being poor. . . . You can't be that poor yourself."

"Hardly," I said. "I have a very rich wife. Haven't you heard?"

"It's not her fault."

"No, it isn't her fault, or is anyone else we know at fault because they have money, it isn't even the money I object to . . ."

"What then?"

"The self-righteousnes, the smugness—if they were only self-made men, then all right. Then perhaps I would have some respect. Then I could go along with the wealth and the ingenuity or the labor which it took to mass it, but everyone we know is living off the fruits of their forefather's wits."

"What is it they say Peter? From shirtsleeve to shirtsleeve in three generations?"

"That's what they say. I don't really give a damn, but I don't have to like them."

"You are just making it hard for yourself."

"No. I am not making it hard enough for myself."

"I don't understand."

"I'll explain some other time. We've got to push on. We still have a drive ahead of us."

We reached Jenner-By-The-Sea at ten o'clock. A small sportfishing community at the junction of the Russian River and the Pacific, Jenner was damp and wrapped in fog.

"We'd better get some coffee," I said. "We've got a rugged stretch ahead."

Cassy nodded and I stopped in front of the only diner remaining open. The owner still remembered me and started a conversation which did not help our situation.

"Mr. Trowbridge, well I declare, bet you don't remember me."

"No, but your face is familiar."

"Used to work for you on the Wolf Ranch, Tile setter."

"That's right, how are you?"

"Finally got to get the missus to see the place . . ."

"Yes, yes," I said and Cassy blushed and nodded.

"Don't know why it took you so long. Ain't a weekend that somebody don't come in here askin' 'bout the place. Really famous 'round here."

Cassy ordered coffee and so did I.

"Lots of architect fellers too, young ones, old ones, told me you got a medal for it."

"That was a long time ago," I said.

"Sure, sure it was. Couldn't lay that tile no more. Didn't even lay it in my own place. How do you like it?"

I looked around the room; it was an old building, a front porch converted to a coffee shop, a counter, several plastic booths in the corner . . .

33

"We got a beer bar in the rear. Ought to see this place at midnight before the sports fishermen get out. Really jumpin'! Yessir . . . Wouldn't care for something to eat?"

"No. Looks pretty socked in. We'd better get moving."

"Good thing you ain't going past Wolf Ranch. They got the highway all dug up . . . hear there's a development going in there."

"Well," I stood, "looks like we'll go on."

"Mighty proud to see you again Mr. Trowbridge. Meet the missus . . ."

"Happy to see you. Good night."

"Take it easy now." He had walked us to the car and looked at the fog with the practiced eye of a coastal dweller. "It's a wet one, sure's a wet one."

I started the engine and carefully threaded the car between the fading white line and the cliffs.

"I'm sorry about that episode."

"What makes you so sure no one else here will recognize you?"

"I told you, there is a brand-new ownership, that man just worked on the project. Besides, you heard him, no one has ever met Mary around here."

"Why *didn't* Mary ever come to see your masterpiece?"

"She doesn't like the ocean."

There were a number of reasons why Wolf Ranch had become an architectural cause célèbre. The utter starkness of the structure in an equally stark environment was unquestionably a breakthrough, the pattern usually having been to ameliorate nature by opposing linearity with curvature, barrenness with the ornate, but there were other factors which played a role. I had designed a number of low-cost housing projects which proved quite pleasing and workable for the tenants, a library at Santa Barbara which delighted the city fathers, in short, a number of projects which kept my name in the forefront professionally, and the Gold Medal that year, though not totally surprising, was still a pleasant accolade from my fellow practitioners.

⌘

THE AWARD was to be made at Wolf Ranch and Mary had carefully planned to see that the children would be properly amused during our three-day absence, her board meetings and car pools were delicately shifted to allow her freedom to accompany me; it was only her sinus, or postnasal drip, that goddamned malady of hers which surfaced for personal convenience, which came into evidence the week before our departure.

I am not certain about the architecture of the sinuses, or better yet, the Danner sinuses, except that I dreamed of them occasionally, thinking of large cavernous holes from which poured millions of gallons of drip, like Niagara, into their respective throats, causing minor wheezing, dyspepsia, a series of minor symptoms not unlike an untuned Diesel engine.

Having been given a week's grace, I genuinely believed Mary. I sent her to Dr. Barton (a man supported solely by the Danner postnasal problems), to be massively treated,

35

but found to my chagrin that he forbade the journey to a cold, inhospitable climate such as surrounds Wolf Ranch.

"I am not asking you to go tonight," I pleaded. "Surely he can cure you by next Friday."

"Even if I *am* well, Peter, Barton thinks that the sea air will only aggravate the sinuses again."

"You mean then, that you're not going."

"I mean, I can't. You know the arrangements I've made. I feel like a fool having to call all the people in the car pool again . . . is it absolutely necessary that *you* go?"

"The Institute awards only one gold medal a year."

"What if *you* were ill?"

"It so happens, I am not."

❧

HIGHWAY ONE is a ribbon of concrete hugging the western edge of the United States like passe-partout around an etching. It parallels the coastline for nine hundred miles from the state of Washington down to Baja, California. The stretch I was now entering traverses perhaps the most spectacular seascape of the Pacific Basin, winding along cliffs in an endless series of hairpin turns, overlooking a vast and treacherous ocean playing itself out against the rugged shore below. There is a constant display of spray and foam, the light of the sun changing the pattern and colors continuously; the dark blue and green of the waves, the granite-gray of the rocks, the whiteness of the spray. At night however, this journey is a frightening experience, for in place of an everchanging seascape there is only an awesome black void, and the presence of fog reduced my speed to the minimum.

Cassy said very little, peering out of the windshield as desperately as I was, following the sweep of the windshield wipers as they cleared and recleared the glass.

"How far is it, Peter?"

"Twenty-two miles."

"All of it like this?"

"All of it."

"Who would ever dream of coming all this way to go to a hotel . . ."

"You sound like Mary."

"I'm sorry."

"Wait till you get there. Wait until you see the view in the morning."

"With this kind of fog I don't expect much of a view at all."

"I've ordered sunshine for tomorrow."

"One bedroom, sunshine, what else have you ordered?"

I understood the implication of the remark but said nothing and concentrated on my driving. I could see the clock on the dashboard; it was eleven and at this pace it would be a good hour before we reached Wolf Ranch.

"Isn't there a place closer Peter?"

"Not on this highway."

"Did you get tired of this road when they were building this place?"

"I loved it. I loved every turn, and every piece of timber that went into the place made it painful because I knew we were getting closer to completion."

"When did you manage all of it?"

"I'd come up Friday nights and leave Monday mornings. Sometimes I brought the kids in the summer. I even wanted to build a cabin here, but Mary would have none of it."

"You must admit it's pretty far."

"From where? Pacific Heights? The Fairmont? Joseph Magnin?"

"My father once had a hunting lodge in Canada," Cassy said. "He and his friends flew up there in a little private plane every fall."

"Did you ever go with him?"

"I was never invited. It was all very male. Years later my mother discovered that they hunted more than deer in Canada. Montreal was a pretty wide-open city in those days . . ." she paused. "Seems funny to be passing judgment on him at this moment when I'm doing the same thing . . ."

"Can't you ever leave Topic One?"

"I'm just not used to this sort of thing, Peter."

"Do you think I am?"

"Well, men feel differently about these things."

"Do they? You once told me they were insensitive."

"I didn't say you were insensitive."

"That's right."

"I'm sorry Peter."

"Forget it. We're just passing Fort Ross."

"Didn't the Russians land there?"

"Yes. Tried to corner the seal market, but they didn't succeed. Still, they left some of the most beautiful architecture around. There's an octagonal house made entirely of timber. No nails. Only wedges. There isn't a carpenter to-day who could build like that."

"You really love your work, don't you?"

"Architecture? Yes. I love architecture. There is so little of it."

"Men are so fortunate. They can plunge their lives into something challenging."

"You can plunge too hard, Cass. There is a difference between diving and drowning."

"I don't know what you mean."

"That's such a marvelous feminine shibboleth."

"What?"

"You men have your work. You can drown yourself in your work."

"Well you do."

"We do what? We have the work, I agree. Most of it is work. Plain ordinary work. Whether you're feeding infants or designing parking lots, it's all work. Not much fun, not terribly stimulating, not overly rewarding."

"At least you have a parking lot when you're finished, or an embassy, or a library. What do I have? A fed child, a made bed, a dusted parlor. . . ."

"Look, Cassy, I know you haven't made too many beds or fed too many children, you've got lots of good help to do that. You have just as much time as Mary to drown your-self in all those wonderful activities we lucky men are in . . . I don't enjoy *drowning* myself in my work at all."

"Then why do you do it?"

"Because there is nothing else."

39

"What would you rather do?"

"Loaf. Read. Make love. To you. How's that? . . . "The fog is lifting—look." I put my arm around Cassy. "We're almost there. I hope you need a drink as badly as I do."

"You'd better keep both hands on the wheel, Peter."

"Yes ma'am." My spirits could not be dampened now.

I passed the lumber mill, the mill workers' cottages, a grocery store, and then we were at Wolf Ranch.

"Safe and sound," I said, but Cassy had already opened the door and did not hear me.

I had patterned my original design of Wolf Ranch around the A-barns indigenous to the area. This would give me a building of sufficient space and height and allow me to eliminate all the ugly appendages normally associated with hotels: kitchens, pantries, laundry rooms, storage houses. I wanted nothing to detract from the stark design of the main house and knew that the seasoned redwood would mellow and weather into the landscape. I kept the entry small and tunnellike, flanked by boulders we had foraged from the beach below. I wanted to dramatize the scope of the main lobby by this intimate entry. The lobby was sixty feet high, one hundred and twenty feet long and seventy feet wide. The fireplace occupied the far wall, a stairway leading to the galleria occupied the wall near the entrance. The owner had wanted to make the hotel seem as uncommercial as possible, and therefore all public areas on the main floor were only separated by levels.

A sunken conversation area flanked the fireplace, another surrounded a small library. A small bar was tucked under the stairwell and a pleasant country kitchen lined another wall. A massive dining table could seat all the guests although they could be served in their own quarters above. There were ten suites off the galleria, each consisting of a living room and a bedroom. All beams were exposed, all bolts and nails left as driven, no material was used that could not be left in its original state.

Only the bedrooms were painted in hues of orange or yellow, the beds covered with white bedspreads, the furniture Mexican and hand-hewn, a hooked rug covered the dark-stained hardwood floor. Large windows faced the ocean below.

I had designed an elongated version of a rolltop desk near the entry which still held only a guest book, a tin cash box used by Wells Fargo a century ago, a bell which Jensen, the owner (a professional musician), said had a pitch of "A" and a small white bowl filled with cornflowers.

Cassy preceded me into the lobby, and I stepped to the desk where a young man had obviously been waiting for us. He was rather curt as I signed the register, but I paused for a minute to look at the great hall and found to my relief that the new owners had apparently not changed things and maintained the property well.

"We welcome you to Wolf Ranch," the desk clerk said somewhat mechanically. "The rates are twenty dollars a night and it includes a bottle of champagne." He reached below the desk and brought out a small bottle of a poor vintage California champagne, gave me the key to Suite Number Four and inquired whether I needed assistance with the luggage. I told him no and he bade me good night and disappeared.

41

Cassy, who had been standing somewhere in the shadows of the one light which was behind the reception desk, had watched all of it, and as I turned to pick up the baggage she preceded me up the stairway, waited until I unlocked the door, turned on the lights in the suite and then followed me in. I put down the suitcase, then the champagne on the dresser.

"Well," I said, "they've added one new touch. The Jensens never gave away a bottle of champagne."

Cassy looked at the bottle, then picked it up. "If ever," she said, "I've been made to feel like a two-bit whore, this is it." She opened the first window she could reach and threw out the bottle of champagne.

I knew the distance that bottle would travel to the beach below and did not expect to hear it crash. I watched her close the window and cross the room.

She sat primly at the edge of the sofa in the living room of our suite and pushed the hair from her forehead.

"I am terribly tired, Peter," she said. "Upset and tired." She stood and walked to the bedroom, then came back to the living room. "Can you manage in here? I just want to go to sleep."

I said nothing and watched her pick up her bag, calmly fold her sweater and go to the adjoining room. She closed the door and then reopened it. "There's no lock on this door. I suppose if you want to use the bathroom in here it will be all right. I'm sorry to be such a stick-in-the-mud." Then she shut the door again.

4

I SAT for an indeterminate amount of time facing the closed bedroom door. I listened to water running in the bathroom, then being shut off. I heard the bathroom door close and I could hear Cassy taking off one shoe, then another, because I recognized the sound of the wooden heels on the wooden floor. I heard the rustling of sheets, a hanger being placed in the closet, the closet door being closed, more rustling of sheets, the propping of a pillow and finally the click of a switch which shut off the light on the night table.

I could not honestly describe my emotions at that point, there were so many. I felt anger, obviously, hatred, frustration. I felt the urge to barge into the bedroom and give Cassy a good beating, I felt adolescent, ridiculous, foolish God knows. Finally I rose, looked about the living room of the suite, my overnight bag near the door, and left the room, half ran down the stairs, found the door which led to the outside, to the water's edge. I walked to the farthest promontory overlooking the ocean. Even in darkness the landscaping looked more manicured than before, the lawn had been freshly mowed, the paths had been rock-edged, but the ocean below me had lost neither its beauty nor its strength. I could see great arches of sea spume in the lazy moonlight as the waves rolled to shore. The noise was deafening and merciful.

There were many things that Cassy could have said. "I'm frightened," she could have said. "I have had second thoughts. [After all these years?] Just hold me. Sit with me. Sit on the bed. Talk to me. Lie in bed with me." Many things, but she had said none of them. "I am tired," she had said. "I am going to bed. Good night." I heard Mary, "Peter, take mother home, I'm tired." "Peter we won't be sailing this weekend, I'm coldish." "Peter we're going to the Deusters tonight. We must . . ."

I walked slowly around Wolf Ranch and somehow its familiarity tempered my mood. I had watched each rock going into place, each beam being whittled to size; I remembered the pitch of the roof and the problems it gave me, the size of the casements, the length of a steel beam.

I was getting chilled and entered the lobby. There was still a good blaze in the fireplace and I stood in front of it warming my hands and my chest. There was little activity in the lobby. An elderly couple sat playing chess, another couple was reading; the only sounds seemed to emanate from a few guests sitting around the little bar tucked under the staircase and I decided to join them.

I sat down and noticed that one of the brass bolts in the stairway had worked itself loose. I asked the bartender whether he had a pair of pliers. He reached under the bar and gave them to me. I fastened the bolt and returned the pliers to him.

"You must be the owner," a young girl sitting at the bar said, apparently having watched me tighten the bolt.

"No, just a guest." I ordered a double martini on the rocks, very dry, a twist of lemon, and sat next to her.

"You certainly have quite a proprietary interest in this place for a guest, or are you just afraid the roof will cave in?"

"The roof has already caved in," I said, not knowing why I said that, "but that bolt bothered me."

"Just like things neat? Everything in its place."

"Not everything, just this place. I designed it."

"Peter Trowbridge," she said.

"Yes."

"My God. Returned to the scene of his triumphs."

"I'd hardly say that."

"I'd hardly *not* say that. Peter Trowbridge, one of three singular figures in American architecture."

"Good heavens, who told you that."

"Frank Lloyd Wright."

"The Master? He told you *that!* How did you know *him?* He's been dead almost ten years."

"I am past puberty . . ."

"Well barely, I don't even know how they serve you a drink."

"My name is Ibsen Iazzo," she extended her hand. "A respectable twenty-six, well-educated, broadly traveled, and you may buy me a drink."

"What are you drinking?"

"I'll have a martini. But a single. You sounded kind of desperate when you ordered."

"Maybe I was. Now tell me about this great figure in American architecture."

"Just like a man aren't you. Love to hear about yourself."

"Not really, I didn't know my name was bandied about like that."

"Bandied indeed! The Master showed slides of your work. I think he had a record of all of it. Wolf Ranch, Trinity Church, Ramo Center, the Embassy in Caracas . . ."

"I never knew that."

"Galbraith once said that modesty was an overrated virtue."

"Yes. He also said something about sodomy in the BMT."

"During the rush hour."

"Yes. During the rush hour. Cheers." We raised our glasses, touched them.

The girl said nothing, only studied me, and I her in return. She had a beautifully chiseled small face: small nose, ears, high cheekbones, rather slanted eyes, neither gray, green nor blue. Her hair which she wore long was the gray-blond of a natural blonde, untouched by bleach, the type of hair blonder at its roots than at the ends. It hung straight from the crown of her head down to her shoulders where it was cut as if chopped off by a guillotine; only one strand, fine and loose, flitted in the air giving some softness to her face which was otherwise rather severe, slightly freckled under the eyes and about the nose. She wore a white turtleneck jersey and black and white houndstooth check hip-huggers cinched below the belly by a narrow black leather belt. He small feet were sandaled in black leather thongs. She was trim, small in the bust, totally flat in the belly, yet her hips gave her some touch of womanhood.

I drank too quickly, I knew, and ordered another round.

"How are you?"

"I'm still good."

"How did you ever get a name like Ibsen?"

"Do you like it?"

"Yes I like it."

"I have been told that when my mother was in labor she somehow remembered some volumes of Ibsen she had checked out of the University library, and rather than concentrating on the job ahead or the joys of impending motherhood she developed a strong fixation about the overdue books . . . somehow this minutiae overshadowed my arrival in this world. So there you have Ibsen. Some of my friends call me I.I."

"Well, it must be nice to have an imaginative mother."

"It is. She's wonderful. Dean of Women at Bryn Mawr. All hustle and bustle and good solid knit suits and a pair of horn-rimmed glasses which slip off her nose. My father left her when I was four and she raised me—alone—beautifully. How's that?"

"And you're an architect?"

"I graduated as an architect, but I am a set designer."

"What a lovely profession. If only more architects were set designers."

"I like it."

47

"What have you designed?"

"A few plays on Broadway, a half a dozen movies. That's why I'm here. Scouting location, it's called."

"You're going to shoot a movie *here?*"

"Yes, dear boy."

"That's terrible."

"Why?"

"I didn't design Wolf Ranch to be the background for some pasty-faced actors."

"Would that really bother you Peter? I'd give you screen credit."

"Bully. You bet it would bother me. The nice thing about Wolf Ranch is that very few people know about it. Those that do treasure that."

"Makes sense you know. I think you're more chauvinistic than the owner. He didn't seem to mind the publicity at all."

I nodded my head. "He's not the original owner. I keep forgetting . . ."

"What are you doing right now?"

"A library for Yale, a research lab for M.I.T., a marina in Baja."

"Why so glum? Those sound like exciting commissions."

"Did I sound glum?"

"You're an unhappy man aren't you?"

I said nothing.

"You are, aren't you," Ibsen persisted. "I saw you arrive earlier tonight. I was sitting by the fireplace. Your wife looked pretty grim."

"That isn't my wife."

"Then what the hell are you doing down here talking to me? Why aren't you safely sacked in upstairs?"

"The lady was tired. I think she said, 'I'm sorry to be a stick-in-the-mud.' "

How could I explain my behavior? I am not a man who normally washes his dirty linen in public. I'm not a whiner, but there was something engaging about this girl, something wide-eyed and honest and open and lovely, and there were the martinis, all those martinis and the thought of Cassy upstairs sound asleep like a good samaritan, and bit by bit I told Ibsen about my escapade, and the talk became more circular as I went on, referring to incidents and people I had talked of before that afternoon, building familiarity out of minutes and hours like drawing plans for a good house, nailing the studs and hanging the curtain walls, fixing a roof, containing, circumscribing. . . .

But there was more than just talk, there was the physical. I remember distinctly her holding my hand in her hands and kissing me first on the cheek and then on the lips, and I remember circling her waist in my arms and our legs getting tangled under the bar, and the bartender feeding new drinks into this union and our hardly having time to drink them and other people at the bar looking away, the bar getting more crowded and intimate and finally Ibsen saying, "Let's go upstairs" and our walking upstairs arm in arm like very young lovers.

I recall the door to Ibsen's room. It was next to Cassy's and mine. And then we were inside and Ibsen undressed very quickly and unashamedly in front of me and she was so beautiful, so very young and childlike and ever so soft and warm and tender.

We had made love for a very long time and it did not feel like the first time at all. Somehow there seemed nothing remiss in all the intimacy, and Ibsen felt like someone I had known another time another place, but I had never known anyone really at all, and after we had made love Ibsen lay across the bed, her head on my shoulder, looking at the ceiling, very quiet and relaxed and I told her that it all had been very good, very good indeed and that I never wanted to leave that room and this bed.

Finally I said, "What am I going to tell Cassy?" I pointed to the room next door.

"Tell her to go to hell. Go get your things, move in and we'll put a DO NOT DISTURB sign on the door. Tell the manager to send in three meals a day and a fresh bouquet of wildflowers in the morning."

"That sounds very simple."

"It is very simple, Peter." Ibsen got off the bed and picked up a book. "Here are one hundred crossword puzzles. Give them to your ex-roommate with my compliments."

"I can't just leave her stranded."

"Why not? That kind of woman thinks men are bastards. Prove it to her. Be a bastard."

"What am I going to tell her?" I sat up myself now and covered myself with a sheet.

"Tell her the truth Peter. Tell her you're sorry things didn't work out last night, and since this was your weekend to play, you've found a new playmate. You want me to tell her?"

"No, no . . . " I wasn't trying to think, but the situation was so ridiculous it was difficult to bring any logic to it at all.

"You think I'm cold and calculating Peter?"

"Anything but that Ibsen. Unique. Let's put it that way."

I lit a cigarette and looked out the window. The first signs of dawn were coming over the ocean. Touches of yellow and orange. . . . It seemed incredulous that all those years of playing games with Cassy, all those nights of some sort of promise of fulfillment should end here, with this girl whom I had known scarcely a hundred minutes, perhaps two hundred minutes, and here we were, bedded, fulfilled, warm, and she unquestioning, unafraid, giving and receiving pleasure with an absolute candor. . . .

I rose and dressed. I tied my necktie and I could see Ibsen still lying in bed, naked, watching me watch her.

"Do you really want to say goodbye Peter?"

"No."

"Then don't. Leave your coat here." She got up quickly and took it in bed with her. "I won't give it up." I made no move to retrieve it and left the room and entered my own suite.

I was startled to see Cassy fully dressed, sitting on the couch, almost poised waiting for me.

"Where the hell have you been?"

"Watch the profanity."

"Oh for Christ's sake . . ."

"Watch it."

"You don't have to tell me Peter. I made the mistake of going down to the lobby looking for you."

"What did you think? I would be sound asleep in one of the Mexican hemp chairs?"

"I didn't know what to think, but I didn't expect you to pick up some cheap broad at the bar."

"Why is every other woman a cheap little broad?"

"Since when do you speak to strange women at bars?"

"You seem to know all about me."

"That horrid manager said, 'Better watch your husband, getting kinda friendly with the ladies . . .'"

I could only laugh.

"I don't think it's very funny."

"No, and I didn't think it was very funny when you slammed the door in my face last night."

"You're right Peter. I was terribly rude. I was trying to find you to apologize."

"And what form would the apology have taken?"

"I don't quite understand."

"Would you have said I am sorry and then we could spend the remainder of the weekend reading quality paperbacks?"

"Are you asking whether we would have gone to bed together?"

"That is precisely what I am asking. What did you think we came here for? Did you think I was a tour guide, or a chauffeur? What?"

"It's all academic now anyway."

"Why?"

"I am sure you must be exhausted after last night."

"Does intercourse exhaust you?"

"I'd rather not talk about it."

"I can believe that."

"The only thing your behavior last night proved, Peter, is that I am glad I went to bed. You're obviously quite practiced at this sort of thing. It took you very little time to find a new friend."

"If you'd like to rationalize your behavior, Cassy, be my guest. If you feel so righteous, why did you find the need to apologize?"

"I really can't remember."

"Well, if you can't remember, I'll remind you."

"I'd just as soon drop the subject."

"I'd just as soon not. I'll be goddamned if I'm going to let you go home feeling like the martyred little housewife."

"What difference does it make what I feel?"

"Only that I wish you or even Mary once could be honest with yourselves. We came here because you suggested the weekend, we've met at Sneaky Pete's because *you* suggested it . . . what was it all about? Tell me, tell me honestly, what was it all about?"

"I didn't want this."

"What is *this*?"

"Bedrooms. Lying about our names, a bottle of champagne."

"What do you honestly think an affair consists of?"

"Friendship, camaraderie . . ."

53

"That sounds like an ad for the Foreign Legion. What about intimacy, warmth, sex? What about sex?"

"Leave me alone," Cassy screamed. "Will you leave me alone?"

"I'll leave you alone, Cassy. How will you get home?"

"I expect you'll take me home."

"I'm sorry. I'm staying."

"You're not staying here with some strange woman you met at a bar."

"I know that strange woman better after one night than I know you after fifteen years."

"You're such a child, Peter."

"I know. Maybe I need a playmate. I have enough mothers already."

Cassy gathered her suitcase and overcoat.

"Can I get you a cab?"

"I can manage."

"Do you need some money?"

"No. I think I'll fly to Arizona. I'm supposed to be there anyway."

I rose and started to leave.

"Peter."

"Yes?"

"Don't forget that we are all invited to the Markhams' Sunday night."

I could only smile. War, famine, epidemics. Nothing took preference over a dinner party in San Francisco.

I returned to Ibsen's room. She looked even lovelier than I had remembered, wearing a simple cotton robe, flowered

54

and prim about the neck. She had ordered breakfast and set a table by the window.

"And then you knew I'd be back."

"No, Peter, I didn't know. Let's say I hoped you'd be back."

"I am."

5

I SAT DOWN on the bed in Ibsen's room and admired her ingenuity in making the little card table festive for breakfast, using a few wild flowers, place cards, a candle which she had swiped from the lobby.

"I have picked a light apéritif," Ibsen said almost mockingly. "In view of a strenuous afternoon I think our systems need much citrus, malt, barley."

"This system, Ibsen, needs a cool kiss on a warm forehead."

"I can oblige you sir." She was coquettish as hell and I put her on my lap.

"Now, now, Peter, I don't want you to think I'm that kind of girl . . . just because I invite you to my room for three or four days, or just because the covers are drawn on that large yummy double bed. . . ."

"No, we'll eat first."

"You *man* . . . Before we do anything at all, Peter, I want to know how you disposed of your friend."

56

"I told her the truth."

"And she accepted it?"

"She was quite elegant. I expected that. I really think she was happy to get out of this situation."

"She wasn't quite so elegant last night."

"Not really. Let's eat. I'm hungry."

We sat at the table and Ibsen lit the candle. I had opened the window slightly and we could hear the sea below us, punctuating our conversation with its own percussion.

"Why aren't you married Ibsen, you seem to be enjoying this domesticity?"

"I do Peter."

I kept the question alive by studying her face rather intensely, but she said nothing for quite a while.

"I *could* give you a simple answer you know."

"What's that?"

"I suppose I didn't want to find myself in the spot you're in right now . . ."

"The barrenness of the middle years, is that what you mean?"

"It happens earlier to a woman. I'm almost there."

"You're twenty-six, Ibsen, that's hardly a tragic age for a girl."

"It isn't, but you see, I'm from a broken home to begin with. I told you my mother's decision to dump my father, his easel and his model when I was only four."

"You didn't mention the model."

"I didn't because she wasn't very important. There's been model after model, poor man, just never will grow up, but these things are never unintentional. My mother as I've told you has always been a headstrong woman. I think she knew she could manage alone: me, her career, herself, anything. It's a sort of self-sufficiency that's almost destructive, and I can't deny that I am privy to that quality."

"She certainly didn't discourage marriage?"

"No, she's too bright for that, but where other families literally groom girls for the bridal bed and the charge accounts, my heritage taught me to use my own resources to grow to be on my own and let marriage enter where it will. I'm not so sure that this is such a wise course."

"You're a beautiful girl, Ibsen."

"Sure. Beautiful, bright, successful, my job pays more money that I know really what to do with, and I'm never really without a man . . . but . . ."

"What?"

"I get involved, often lightly, sometimes deeply, I'm modern, you've got *proof* of that, I don't believe in the tyranny of sex, I like it, but there's always a point, a hairy leg, or a twitch, or manner of speaking, sometimes a wife, or an irresponsibility, always something which I magnify and magnify until the thought of marriage to *that* man looks dreary . . . I get frightened. I back out. Change the phone number . . . disappear. . . . Is your wife pretty Peter?"

"I couldn't tell you what she looks like," I said quite honestly.

"I can believe that, Peter. I really wasn't being nosy. I just wanted to confirm something."

"What?"

"I think really that people in the aesthetics business, architects, artists, become somewhat blasé about anatomy."

"Count me out."

"Come on really Peter, I'm hardly a raving beauty."

"Not fair," I said.

"What's not fair?"

"You can't define my sense of aesthetics."

"I get a pretty good clue from your work."

"Well . . ."

"I'm complimented . . . but what else could you say?"

"Would you like to hear my analysis of your physiognomy?"

"Why not? Should I undress?"

"No, my memory is pretty good."

"You don't like to see me naked?"

"Wait until after breakfast."

"Man!"

We played like this for hours. Half fun, half revelations, we ran out of firewood and I sent down to get more. It was past eleven in the morning when I stood up and felt the pains of limbs gone numb and a head too light and happy to control them. I stumbled and fell on the bed and Ibsen lay next to me.

"You never did tell me about my looks."

All right, disrobe, and I'll get out my magnifying glass."

"Peter Trowbridge, I am *small* in the bust, but not that small."

"Let's start right there," I said, "I happen to like small busts. . . ."

We had succeeded in keeping the morning from becom-

59

ing too alcoholic and I reveled in our lovemaking more than I had the previous night. However many men Ibsen had slept with she still seemed to manage a certain excitement, but perhaps it was my kind of excitement, no swearing, panting, lusting, just a certain mutuality, a feeling that her head tucked well under my arm or my face on her back felt cool, and all of it like this afternoon felt natural.

Ibsen went to sleep and I watched her slowly gain independence in that bed, but I lay awake, even rose and lit a cigarette, sat in front of the dying fire in the living room of our quarters and watched a fishing boat fight the currents below Wolf Ranch.

◦◦◦◦◦

I HAD just turned forty, and whether that chronological milestone produced enough trauma or whether sheer desperation was the motivation, I don't know, and still I found it amusing that where other men were keeping women half their ages, spending middays in barren motel rooms, drinking hard double martinis and screwing their guts out, the only clandestine activity I could point to were thrice-weekly visits to Dr. Gerlehen.

It amused him at first that I insisted on paying cash for his time to preclude discovery, and finally this foible hardened into yet another reason to change the pattern of my life.

He was a tweedy, older man, anecdotally Jewish, kind, warm, his office plain, rather tasteless touches of Las Vegas Baroque, a gilt mirror, white carpeting, framed poor reproductions of Manet and Cézanne on the walls, but the ordinary physical surroundings quickly became irrelevant as I saw his careful unfolding of my psyche like unwrapping a crated box of Tiffany glassware. He was methodical and precise, meticulous in detail without prying, tactful and yet provocative.

Of course I was a victimized human being. The Nazis, stern parents, a hostile new country, Mary, Mary's parents and their wealth, even my own children and *their* innate independence. It was all there. Quite obvious; although the reasons for victimization were not so clear.

I was a good-looking man. I was talented. Successful. I had my share of honors. I was a decent person. I paid my taxes. I was charitable. Why? Why? What was the need for self-flagellation? A touch of voyeurism? Bedwetting? Masturbating? Castration complex? Overt homosexuality? What was it? I wanted answers I complained, and I could describe the subtlety of a given situation. I was perceptive, and I knew texture and feel and smell and the innuendo of a raised eyebrow or the meaning of an inflection, but I *was* crippled by the Germanicism of my puritanical upbringing. I could not speak of sperm or cunt or jerking off, or coming too soon or too late or not at all. I could not confess to anything which seemed prurient or aberrant.

I knew what he was doing. If I described intercourse with Mary he would be clinical; he would be painfully, brutally clinical. How well I remembered.

"You mean she makes you fondle her labia?"

"Yes."

61

"Up and down or sideways?"

"She tells me."

"How?"

"Up. Down. Up down, sideways. There, no up, up. There."

"Does she get moist then? . . . Does she?"

"I don't know."

"You must know."

"I guess she does."

"Then what does she do?"

"I put my finger in her vagina."

"Your finger?"

"Yes."

"And what is she doing about you?"

"What do you mean?"

"Does she hold you?"

"No."

"Does she play with your penis?"

"No."

"Does she hold it?"

"No."

"Your scrotum?"

"No."

"Your buttocks?"

"No."

"You lie there and fondle her like a sycophant?"

"Yes."

"And when do you enter her vagina?"

"When she tells me."

"What does she say?"

"Now."

"Now?"

"Yes."

"Now darling. Now, please?"

"No. Now!"

"And she reaches a climax?"

"I suppose."

"Do you?"

"Sometimes."

"What happens when you don't?"

"I take a shower."

"Do you always take a shower, after intercourse?"

"Yes."

"Why?"

"I don't know."

"What do you mean you don't know. Why do you usually take a shower?"

"It refreshes me."

"From what?"

"I feel dirty, grimy, sticky."

"All right, Mr. Trowbridge," he would say, and the hour would be over.

I would get up and pay him.

"Still haven't told your wife that you are coming?"

"No."

He would shake his head, half amused, half puzzled, and would see me to the door.

∽∾∾

I HAD made love to Ibsen. I had held her and played with her and she with me. I had touched her, kissed her, my lips, my tongue exploring her body. I felt her climax and my own, her musculature embracing me. I tasted her and felt my legs covered by her wetness and my own, and I had loved it. There was no urge to shower, no urge to cleanse, there was stickiness between us and I cherished it, there were odors and I loved them. I, too, fell asleep, happy, feeling a curious abandon, slightly puzzled. . . .

6

THERE WERE three or four freckles about Ibsen's nose which were quite prominent and lovely. They somehow reminded me of a Calder mobile because her face was never quiet, her facial muscles were as alive as the rest of her, and so these mustard-colored spots, these small areas of liver-colored confetti were constantly in motion and acted, perhaps for me a man who *likes* freckles, as a continuous source of amusement. I can quite easily document this, because when I awoke late in the afternoon, Ibsen was sitting at the foot of our bed, wearing my T-shirt and nothing more, her legs in a most indecorous position, and still I could see nothing but the freckles on her nose.

I was in a wonderful humor. I remember saying, "This may sound strange to you my love, Ibsen."

"Yes?"

"But somehow I don't know where I am."

"I see."

"You don't see, you see, I should be in bed next door,

with my old old flame Cassy, instead of my old old wife Mary, now do you see?"

"You are, Peter Trowbridge, I've been sitting here thinking a very dirty old man."

"Good."

"And I would like to know whether you can make love before you've brushed your teeth?"

"No."

"Good for you. Well I've already brushed mine, and I've squeezed one solid inch of Colgate on your multi-tufted beauty in the bathroom."

"I can see you're an absolute wastrel, no man needs more than one half an inch."

"How do you feel, lover?" Ibsen asked.

"Marvelous. I feel so good Ibsen, I am going to get up, brush my teeth and then . . ."

"Yes?"

"I'm going to do my Canadian Air Force exercises."

"Well—"

"Well what . . ."

Ibsen pushed me back on the bed. "I don't give a darn if you're suffering from b.o. or h.a. or galloping psoriasis, I'm not letting you out of bed."

"Wouldn't you like to take a nice brisk walk?"

"No."

"Would you like me to find a lovely intimate restaurant?"

"No."

"Take our shoes off and wade into the sunset?"

"No."

"Just lie here and make love and love and love . . ."

"Yes."

"Hmmmm."

Ibsen propped her face on her hand. "This idyll won't go on forever. This is our last day."

"Tell me, Ibsen, will I just be another one of those numbers in your life?"

"Not you, Peter. You are Peter Trowbridge for me. Peter Trowbridge in the midst of a bad affair. Peter Trowbridge at Wolf Ranch."

"Do you have everyone classified like that?"

"There weren't countless thousands you know Peter."

"That's reassuring."

Ibsen looked at me, somewhat sheepishly. "Why should that be reassuring to you?"

"Good question . . . why should it? Can you just put this right out of your mind like shuffling a deck of cards and coming up with a new face card?"

"What difference does it make Peter?"

I rose and played aimlessly with the fireplace poker.

"What difference does it make . . ."

"Yes."

"You will return to middle-class morality, and I shall return to the swinging life of the bachelor girl."

"You don't sound as convincingly flippant as you'd like."

"What difference does it really make what I sound like?"

"It makes a difference to me. Both parties shook hands manfully and patted each other on the back for being so thoroughly modern."

"What are you driving at, Peter?"

"There's got to be more."

"How much more can there be? We met. We loved. You're a much-married man. What else do you want of me?"

I put my head in my hands and closed my eyes. "You're very right, Ibsen. Where are you going from here?"

"To Nice."

"*Nice?*"

"Yes, Nice . . ."

"That's pretty far."

"From what?"

I wasn't looking at Ibsen, I remember.

"You want to come? Nice is lovely this time of the year. Deep clouds over the Mediterranean. Warm, soft lovely nights."

"Stop it."

"Couldn't you take one week out of your life, Peter?"

I fell back on the bed, my arms outstretched. I looked at the ceiling.

"A week. My God, a whole week."

"Is that so impossible?"

"I don't even have enough money to get to Europe."

"I thought you were a rich man."

"I am, I suppose. I must be worth a million dollars."

"It doesn't cost all that much, you know."

"You don't seem to understand. Everything is done with checks. My salary, everything just ends up in the Chemical Bank of New York."

"Then write a check."

"Mary countersigns all the checks."

"How can you live like that?"

68

"You wouldn't believe me, Ibsen, but until this very minute, it never really made a damned bit of difference. I have never been much for acquiring things."

"Don't you ever get the urge to spend money frivolously? Isn't there something your little heart desires?"

"I buy three suits at Bullocks and Jones in January and a sport coat and slacks in May. I get a new automobile every three years from the firm, my tobacco is delivered bimonthly from Dunhill in New York and I own a forty-foot sloop-rigged sailboat called the *Pinata*, otherwise known as Father's Folly."

"And you are not fooling me one bit, Peter Trowbridge."

"What do you mean?"

"You have three Gold Medals from the AIA, the youngest architect in the American Academy of Arts and Sciences, you have given more visual pleasure to more people . . . come on, I won't buy that 'I am really a very simple sort of man' philosophy at all."

" 'Didn't you win some sort of medal for that place?' Cassy asked me yesterday on our way up here."

"Some sort of medal, Peter Trowbridge, you are an idiot to cavort with that sort of woman."

"At least you girls are consistent in your mutual admiration."

"Some sort of medal. Where do you keep it? Where do you keep all three of them?"

"I don't know."

"They're not on display? They're not hung in the library?"

"No, they're not on display."

69

"Your children don't run around and show them to their friends?"

"My children don't show them to their friends."

"I wish I had a week to straighten you out."

I stood and stretched my arms.

"What now?"

"I'm going to take a walk, Ibsen."

"Can I come?"

"No."

I started for the door, but Ibsen stopped me.

"Sit down for a minute."

"Yes?"

"I, I . . ."

"What?"

"I don't want you to make any decisions that you really don't want to make."

"You mean you don't want to be responsible."

"That is exactly what I mean. I'll be responsible for myself."

"When you return from Nice where will you be?"

"In Sausalito. There's where I live."

"Can I see you then?"

"No. No hiding Peter. No meetings after the rush hour. What for? I don't need it."

"You don't. What if I come to Nice?"

"We'll have a week."

"I know we'll have a week. Then what?"

"Why don't we cross that bridge when we come to it?"

7

I WALKED OUT of Wolf Ranch, past guests loading their cars in the parking lot, a gardener mowing the lawn and ambled aimlessly down the highway.

Around the bend of the road was a sawmill which had supplied most of the lumber during the building of Wolf Ranch. It was apparently still in operation for I could smell the good pungent odors of freshly cut redwood. I walked to the open shed which housed the huge circular saw and watched eight men gently guide a giant redwood along the carriage to the blade. They were short, dark, heavyset men of Russian or Polish extraction; still they had the agility of men used to handling heavy materials and machines.

They worked methodically and took no notice of me as I walked about the compound of the sawmill. Six simple frame houses, not unlike the kind used by railroad personnel, were scattered about the grounds. They were neat houses surrounded by small gardens tended with great care.

A steam whistle blew and I watched the men from the mill walk to their homes for the noon meal. Two small boys, lean and dark, sat on a pile of freshly cut lumber, as wordless as their elders, and they too jumped to the ground and ran to one of the cottages. The entire scene seemed reminiscent of a Welsh coal mining town I had once visited during the war on an idyllic weekend spent in the country, and I felt a touch of nostalgia and envy, for those lives seemed so simple and well-organized, a rather paradoxical state of mind considering the proposition Ibsen had just made.

The year was 1936 and I was twelve years old standing at the rail of the S.S. *California* entering San Francisco Bay. It was a clear January day and I recall the American passengers fervently straining to see Alcatraz where Al Capone was at the time, ignoring all the beauty of the bay and the city bordering it. I stood between my parents, all of us visibly downcast after two months at sea. We had emigrated from Germany, and San Francisco was our last port of call.

I can even recall my father's speech the night we had departed from Hamburg. "We are going on a long ocean voyage," he said. "Enjoy it. It will be many years before you'll go on such a cruise again." I watched the tugs join the ship and gently head it to its mooring, and I watched the fog creep through the Golden Gate, and when time arrived for debarkation, the sky was gray and moist, the atmosphere leaden and somewhat frightening.

A handful of my mother's distant relatives met us at the

dock and, after a hearty meal in a waterfront restaurant, drove my family to a one-room apartment. It was a shabby, poorly furnished room; a bowl of fruit stood on the counter in the kitchen, the cupboards were filled with canned goods, a good samaritan had brought a bottle of wine, but it was not until all the friends and relatives had departed and my father had opened the closet door and pulled down an ancient double bed which almost filled the room, it was not until then that I watched my parents sit on that bed, almost fearful of catching some dread disease from its moth-eaten blankets, and cried.

The loss of their home, their worldly goods, the loss of their friends and homeland had all fused with the mixture of excitement and urgency to leave that politically hostile land. Even the long boat trip, past South America through the Panama Canal, had somehow shielded them from the reality of their plight. It was now, only now, sitting penniless and jobless on that pull-down bed, that they truly felt like immigrants.

My mother had heated a can of pork and beans and my father had opened the bottle of wine. We drank it out of thick, viscous jelly glasses, I can recall, and I fell asleep on an ancient couch. It was my first day in America.

I watched the last of the lumbermen's children enter their little houses and left the compound. I walked aimlessly and finally sat on an abandoned bench overlooking the sea. It was getting chilly. There was more gray in the water than blue.

·

73

We had gone to Stuttgart for our physical examination to get our visa to the United States and sat for five hours in a drafty hallway until our names were called. The examination was cursory: our ears, eyes and hearts were checked like so much cattle being bought at auction, and then there were more hours of waiting, careful, measured unprotesting waiting until a rubber stamp buried itself in an inkpad and came crashing down on the visa. Three times the rubber stamp came down, imprinting the Seal of the United States of America on three long white pieces of paper. Three signatures were affixed, and it was not until we had reached a little park a mile from the consulate that my father gave voice to his exultation. We had been delivered. We had a passport to the Promised Land. That had been thirty-two years ago. Sitting here, on this crude bench, debating whether to return to the Continent, I wondered about my father's earlier exultation, wondered whether I was like a refugee again, or like a refugee still, wondered whether I was leaving home or returning.

I watched a cab pull up to the hotel and saw Cassy step in. There was a moment's pause and then the cab departed passing the spot where I was sitting. I did not look up to see Cassy's face and hoped she had not spotted me. That too would now end; she would return to San Francisco with renewed fervor to dignify that insensitive union of hers. She had had her fling and could now settle comfortably into middle age, couching her miseries and desires in virtue and hard work, and though after one night with Ibsen, little freckle-nosed Ibsen, it mattered little to me what happened to Cassy. I knew that even that promise, no matter how nebulous it had been over the years, would remain unfulfilled, and if I could talk to Mary, if I could *ever* have talked to Mary, she would say, grow up Peter, it is time you grew up, when are you going to grow up? but somehow now, this very minute, this *one* hour knowing that Ibsen was packing, that she was leaving here, and me, made me question, honestly question the equation that maturity equaled misery.

"I'm coming," I said. "I'm coming along."

Ibsen was packed, her suitcases by the door. She was wearing a simple, quite elegant houndstooth-check suit, a white blouse, her accessories alligator and expensive. I pushed her toward the bed.

"I think," I said, "that a man planning to accompany you halfway around the world deserves a kiss."

"You deserve more than that, do you think we have time?"

"You're a nymphomaniac."

"I told you so . . ."

"How much money do you think I'll need?"

"How are you going to get money?"

"I remembered I have a check in my wallet. We each carry one. Mary and I."

"For internment in case of accidental death."

"Something like that."

"I don't know Peter. One week. How about fifty thousand dollars?"

"Don't joke."

"I'm not joking. Some of that loot must be yours."

"You're not only a nymphomaniac, but a gold digger."

75

"*And* a homewrecker. Remember what the lady said."

"Yes. A homewrecker. Let's get out of here. I've got to buy some clothes . . . get my passport. When do we leave?"

"Midnight tonight. We'll be in Copenhagen tomorrow."

"Ibsen, do you realize what I am doing?"

"Yes, you're going to Europe for a week with a nymphomaniac."

"That's not what I'm talking about."

"I know what you are talking about. Don't get heavy darling, there will be time to talk."

"I'm not so sure."

"Here, Peter," Ibsen wrote on a scratch pad, "here is the name of a little bar in Sausalito. I'll meet you there in four hours. Drive carefully, and if you change your mind, come by and buy me a drink anyway."

8

I KNEW that Mary would be perplexed. Angry perhaps when she would receive a call from Chicago stating I would be gone another week. I had been away from home before, of course. Commissions had taken me all over the country, but it had always been organized, Mary had been able to adjust our social life, the parties and the receptions: "Then you will return Friday noon, that is good because we must go to the Websters for supper." Somehow grudgingly my career existed as far as Mary was concerned but it was a nuisance. There was a life outside of business, there was something she was pursuing which had very little to do with reality, or perhaps I was unwilling to face reality. Mary did not depend on me for her sustenance. She was a rich woman in her own right. A rich woman in her own right. How often have I heard that phrase?

I drove quickly, ignorant of the scenery. Somehow I wanted nothing to disturb my decision and wished the momentum of the weekend would not let up. I did not want to think, to rationalize. Should I phone Mary? Should I phone the children? Did I have the right to pursue Ibsen? What of the end of the week? No. No. I spoke to myself. Think! Go to your office. Cash a check. Buy some clothes, a ticket, luggage, what about travel insurance? To whom should I mail the policy? What about the office? What about the work in progress?

A week. One week. One goddamn week. I could be ill for a week. Mary would suspect nothing. Nothing. She would wonder why I didn't call, but she would suspect nothing—what a hollow victory. I turned on the car radio, but it made me more nervous, and I switched it off again. I adjusted the seat and the rear-view mirror, opened the window, closed it, but finally I could see Sausalito, and then I found our rendezvous, a tiny little bar overlooking the yacht harbor. Ibsen was waiting.

"You drive too fast," I said.

"Impetuous youth," she said, pushing a martini my way. "Are you saying hello or goodbye?"

"Is there an earlier plane for Copenhagen?"

"No, my love. Are you quite certain about what you're doing Peter?"

"No. I'm only quite certain I don't want to say goodbye. I've got a million things to do," I said.

"So do I, Peter. I want you to see my apartment before you leave. Will you follow me?"

Ibsen drove along the waterfront and then climbed into the hills of Sausalito. We stopped finally at an old Victorian house. Ibsen got out of her car and said, "Come in for a minute."

It was a good small apartment and displayed the kind of taste I expected of Ibsen. The floors were dark, polished hardwood, the severity relieved occasionally by colorful throw rugs. The walls and most of the furniture were white; only the etchings, the rubbings, the posters and little three-dimensional set designs covered the walls. There was a small porch and a good view, of the bay of Sausalito, a few oriental plants covered the redwood railing. Her French provincial bedroom was softer than the rest of the house: a canopied bed, blue-and-white striped bedspread, an antique commode, a small chair covered with petit point that stood in front of a small Franklin stove. I looked about Ibsen's quarters carefully and I knew that she wanted me to.

"There *is* a home," she said, "and some semblance of order and stability in my life."

"So there is," I said.

"I wanted you to see that, Peter, come here, I'll show you something!" She took me by the hand and led me to the small hallway leading to the kitchen. The walls were covered with photographs, perhaps twenty or thirty, all beautiful and unrelated. There among them were architectural renderings of Wolf Ranch and a church I had done in Topeka.

"You see, darling, you are enshrined."

"I'm moved."

Ibsen shoved me toward the door. "You'd better move. We've got a lot of traveling ahead of us."

"I'll buy some pajamas."

"Baby blue. You'll look adorable."

"Baby blue."

"With white piping."

I kissed her, and left. It was only a short drive from Sausalito over the Golden Gate Bridge, the fog shrouding the towers.

❧

MARY AND I had two houses, one in Pacific Heights, which we bought after the birth of our first child, the second one in Atherton, a summer house set in a wooded grove in the Danner compound. I had designed this house myself, and it was a successful structure, yet with both these ample residences I coveted the small apartment Ibsen had just shown me. Whether it was the very confinement, the womb-like quality much like the cabin of my boat, or the fact that it was a place she could call her own, it represented something I very much needed.

It would be unfair to say that Mary actually made me consciously aware of what she was contributing financially to our marriage. She did not refer to our house as *her* house, but still the money gave her a certain independence, a distinct veto power. She would say, "The living room needs new drapes. I am going to call Sloans tomorow." There would be no discussions, no questions, no juggling of funds. She made the decision, she had the money and though I had seen a number of marriages torn apart by money problems, the very absence of the problem was also castrating. There was nothing really we aspired to, nothing we scrimped and saved to acquire. She was not disparaging about the earnings of my practice, but my efforts were really inconsequential. We could survive without my working.

❦

I PHONED Tony Wang, one of my partners, and asked him to meet me at his apartment. Tony and I had spent most of our school years together and since he was recently divorced and lived alone, I felt it would be easiest, of all my other partners, to make him my confidant.

He lived in a small flat on Telegraph Hill, a rather barren series of rooms displaying oriental frugality and showing signs of his recent marital turmoil. He was waiting for me when I arrived.

"Hi Peter. I thought you were in Chicago."

"So does everyone else."

"Then you weren't in Chicago?"

"No. But I'll confuse you even more. I'm leaving for Europe tonight."

"Why?"

"A girl."

"I don't know what to say."

"Say nothing."

"I don't mean to say that I'm not happy for you."

"I know that."

"I've known you for a long time Peter, but I've never understood your private life."

"I've never understood it too well myself."

"I believe that. Would you like some coffee? A drink?"

"I'll take some coffee."

"Is this serious Peter? Has it been going on a long time?"

"I've only met her and I can't tell you how serious it is."

"Serious enough to go to Europe obviously."

"For a week."

"I am really not trying to pass judgment, Peter."

"I know that, I know that."

"I've screwed up my own life so completely, I'm the last person that should say anything."

"I felt that you would help me."

"Of course, what can I do?"

"I've got to cash a check."

"How much do you need?"

"Five thousand dollars. I'll give you a personal check. Take it out of the firm. I need traveler's checks, and my passport which is in the safe. Also . . ."

"Yes?"

"I'm not phoning Mary. Someone will phone her from Chicago. She'll probably call the office. Just cover for me. Tell her I'm on a special job for the State Department. Something. Anything."

Wang nodded. "I can handle it. Who else knows?"

"No one. The less commotion the better."

"I agree. What do you need?"

"I'd like to take a shower. Take a nap."

"Make yourself at home."

"Thank you."

Wang was quiet and circumspect, but perhaps I wanted to talk about Ibsen, my trip, perhaps for my own needs.

"I am going to Europe because of a girl," I said. "Old stodgy Peter Trowbridge with the short sideburns and the Brooks Brothers suit."

"Someone you've known a long time?"

"Forty-eight hours."

"All of them spent in bed," Wang said, not questioning.

"Practically all of them. She's bright, beautiful, warm, she's an architect, as a matter of fact, but she designs sets."

"Are you planning to divorce Mary?"

"I'm planning a week, Tony. For me, that's pretty good."

"What happens at the end of the week?"

"I don't know, I really don't know; it was either this week or the end of the affair. The decision seemed quite simple."

"If that one was simple, perhaps the next one won't be so difficult."

"Perhaps."

I drew no sparks from Wang. I knew neither whether he was critical or benign about my adventure.

"What do you think?"

"I think it's high time. For a man of your talents I've never been able to comprehend your pedestrian life style. You can't pour all your love into your work."

"It's insane, I know. It's all insane."

"Why? What is sanity? I've been married three times, divorced three times, I've been happy and unhappy, but I've been *one* of the two. Go, Peter, the world won't fall apart."

"It's only a week."

Wang nodded, then rose. "You want five thousand dollars in traveler's checks. You'll have to sign those."

"I know. Have somebody from the bank bring them over."

"How are you getting to the airport?"

"By cab."

"I'll take you."

"I'd appreciate that."

Wang left the apartment. I looked at my watch. I had eight hours before my plane departed and I knew this voluntary confinement would prove painful. I found a blanket and a pillow in the hall closet and tried to sleep on the couch, but sleep would not come. Three lives, Mary's and the children's, were inextricably intertwined in mine, three people unaware of my presence in their midst and unaware of my plans to go to Europe. "Are you going to get a divorce?" Wang's question seemed so blunt, and yet, why should it shock me?

I looked about the apartment which, by compounding the purity of the Orient with bachelorhood gave it a dreadfully barren appearance.

The cupboards would be bare, I knew, the refrigerator held only mixers and beer, the closets held well-pressed shirts and sports jackets. Somewhere would be skis and somewhere else Tony's photo equipment.

It was depressing, and yet made me wonder whether this is what I was opting for. Would such quarters be my alternative to a well-run, orderly tasteful home where meals were served on time and a laundress took care of linens and a man washed windows twice a month?

But how barren was my own life really? How much of

my house was *mine*? The bedspread on which I couldn't sit? The study which I couldn't litter, how much of *me* was in that house? An umbrella stand in the hall, a Persian rug in my study, a Brancusi in the dining room?

The messenger arrived from the bank and I signed the checks, stacking them neatly on Tony's coffee table after he had departed. I felt like a thief when I put them in my pocket and poured myself a drink. I tried once more to bury my head in the corner of the couch but all the demons of guilt and self-incrimination kept me awake.

There had been other opportunities to change the course of my life. Ten years ago I had been offered the position of consulting architect for the United Nations and four years later the Assistant Deanship at Yale, both challenging admirable opportunities, but somehow Mary prevailed.

Nothing seemed worthwhile enough to change her mode of living in San Francisco, and nothing would make me give an ultimatum.

What was it then which let me make the decision to accompany Ibsen so freely, to toy with such frivolity when I avoided serious steps in my career? Perhaps my life and Mary's would have been the same. Whether New York or New Haven, it would have been a different house, and different school for the children, but how different would it really have been?

My father had been close to fifty years of age when we had come to America in 1936. Fifty years old, ten dollars in his pockets, and all the worldly goods one sturdy suitcase would hold. It was a barren land, wracked by depression;

able native citizens were roaming the streets looking for work. My father was a fine-looking well-trimmed man, his manners courtly and old worldish, and after six months of agony he found a position as a floorwalker in a department store. I recalled the night he received his first paycheck and he had taken my mother and myself to a small Basque restaurant in the Tenderloin district of San Francisco. It had been a long time since we had a fresh crisp loaf of French bread and even longer that my parents had enjoyed a carafe of red wine, but I don't know why I was intent on flagellating myself at this point. My parents were no longer starving. True, they were not affluent, but they were healthy and secure. My children were living not one whit differently than if I were at the office, and Mary, save for the news of my absence, was surely tending her own garden very nicely.

I had felt no overwhelming guilt about leaving with Cassy for the weekend. Perhaps she was right, we weren't going to hurt anyone. I am not so certain what I really expected even if Cassy had allowed me to go to bed with her; I would have enjoyed it, and yet it was more a question of a fait accompli rather than a turning point. It seemed quite reasonable that we would be able to return home to our respective lives; perhaps the experience might have led to future meetings, but I felt no threat with Cassy. I did with Ibsen.

I looked at my watch. It was five o'clock and I took a long, leisurely shower, drowning my guilts and my concerns in steaming hot water, washing my hair, scrubbing my back with a long-necked brush and finally toweling my body until the skin tingled and felt alive. I shaved and brushed my hair, I trimmed some stray hair in the lobes of my ears and in my nostrils, packed my newly bought clothes in an overnight bag and finally made another drink, but mercifully Tony returned from the office and helped pass the remaining hours before departure. He was both helpful and masculinely restrained in his questions, it was only I who persisted in looking for condemnation for my actions.

"I am alone with my work," Tony explained. "I am alienated from my family who were born and still live spiritually in the Orient. I've had no room for women, really, or a family. I've been through three wives, you know that Peter."

"Yes."

"And I keep looking for something I find really only in myself."

"But you keep looking."

"Yes, but I'm not very pleased with that either. But you are a loner too, Peter."

"With a wife and two children."

"Yes," Wang perused. "A wife and two children. We have been partners for fifteen years. I think I have seen Mary twice during that period."

"She hasn't forgiven you yet for that wedding supper on the *Tiburon*."

"Good God, does she still talk about that?"

"Only when she's angry."

"Why can you only stay one week?"

I stood up and laughed. "Come on you immoral bastard, get me to the airport. You bachelors are all the same."

"How's that?"

"You want company. You want to shore up your own insecurities."

"I, Mr. Trowbridge, am at peace with myself. *You* are asking for absolution."

"Quite right. Isn't there some sage oriental bit of wisdom to tide me over these perilous times?"

"There is, no doubt some oriental bit of wisdom, but I think some occidental female will tide you over well enough."

9

THERE IS something intriguing and mysterious about an international airport in the evening hours. Perhaps the overtones of danger of the imminent flight or the diminution of man in relation to the giant airplanes, perhaps the high-domed waiting rooms, the hushed voices, the great expanses of glass and burnished steel, the trim little girls and the lean young men, the quiet toasts in the eternally dark cocktail lounges, the endless changing pattern of humanity departing and arriving, but all of this swept me up into that kaleidoscope and I was grateful, for once more I was forced to live by signs, by arrows, by a code. Check in, baggage, customs, immigration. Sign here, step to the counter, place your luggage on the scale. May we see your passport, your ticket, your evidence of immunization? Step to the right, to the left . . .

Though I was early I looked for Ibsen under the clock at the SAS counter, but she had not yet arrived. I felt free and unencumbered of my luggage, holding only my new raincoat, still somewhat stiff and boxy, over my arm. I patted my chest and felt my passport, my round-trip ticket. Flight Number 1. Copenhagen, Nice and return.

I bought a newspaper and cigarettes at the newsstand and sat in a shadowy corner of the terminal which would let me observe Ibsen's arrival. I bought a small bouquet of African violets from the florist who lovingly enveloped them in a paper doily, admiring her handiwork by stretching out her arm and looking at the flowers, then handing them to me as if I had made the wisest of decisions. I scanned the paper casually, but the troubles of the world seemed very distant this evening. I could rouse neither passion for a South American revolution or the imminent censure of a legislator. People had troubles, so did nations. It was a sage and sanguine outlook; I knew I was using the paper only as a prop until Ibsen arrived.

She stood under the clock at the appointed time and I was startled by her beauty. She was trim and looked even younger than I had remembered, wearing a well-cut blue knit suit, a red-and-blue polka-dotted scarf tied artfully around her neck, her white gloves sparkling, her hair the color of well-scrubbed teak, her eyes a violet blue, her legs so thin and shapely and tanned. I jumped up, as if ordered, leaving the paper, even the flowers and my raincoat, and half ran to embrace her.

"Did you think I would make it, darling?"

"I'd hoped you wouldn't ask that question."

"Why?"

"Because either answer would condemn me."

"Well did you?"

"I'm happy you are here darling, I really am."

"That's good enough."

"You've left your raincoat and some flowers on that bench."

"So I have." I retrieved them but did not give Ibsen the flowers immediately.

"Are they for me?"

"They are for the captain, actually, but you may hold them."

We boarded the plane and I was relieved to find no one I knew aboard; it was quite empty really and Ibsen and I were able to share an entire row of seats in the rear of the airplane.

"It seems strange to take such a long journey without anyone saying goodbye."

"You get used to that," Ibsen said. "It's even worse when you travel alone. Somehow you never get blasé about these vast distances, the time changes."

The cabin door was finally shut and I could hear the jets being started one by one, effortlessly, and then we were taxiing down the runway, past a series of multicolored lights; it reminded me of Christmas and having a toy train set up, running it in the dark, the tiny headlights of the locomotive casting a tiny beam on the track ahead.

The cabin lights were dimmed, the stewardess fussed over the passengers, checking seat belts, hand luggage, handing out little pillows, blankets; and then as the engines built up power, I felt the plane straining at the leash until the brakes were released and power overcame inertia, until motion became more motion and we were airborne. I felt Ibsen's hand in mine as I watched San Francisco drop below us and we headed out over the Pacific. I was grateful that she said nothing during our takeoff and remained quiet until the pilot greeted the passengers over the intercom. He projected good weather for our flight, gave our expected arrival time, and stated that the temperature in Copenhagen was 58 degrees at present.

"It's incredible. We've barely cleared the runway and the pilot is already projecting the weather in Copenhagen."

"It's the next stop, lover."

"So it is."

There was a full moon and its reflection on the wing of the airplane cast a pale-blue light into the cabin.

"Just look at that wing, Ibsen. Isn't that a beautiful shape?"

"You lectured at Aspen once about that subject didn't you?"

"How did you know?"

"I read about it somewhere. What did you say?"

"I have, believe it or not my love, spent most of my professional life trying to determine *why* architecture on the whole is so poor. For a dispassionate man this has been a religion."

"We can debate that later."

"The religion?"

"No, the passion."

"All right, but one day I was single-handing the *Pinata*, a mean feat of seamanship I may add, and I wondered why man could design as beautiful an object as a sailboat and fail so miserably in housing. It was a question which obsessed me until I realized that every single component in a sailboat has a reason."

"Form follows function?"

"That is an oversimplification. Form follows function, true, but one of the primary functions of a sailboat is motion. The function of an airplane is motion; a balloon, a bicycle, all in themselves beautiful objects, all of them designed by man. True?"

"True."

"Now you will say, you cannot give a house wings, or put it on wheels, you cannot make it float. It is not designed for motion. It does not move forward, upward, sideways, downward, it is actually the antithesis of motion. Antimotion. It must be firm, secure, rooted; it must withstand heat and cold, the sun, the winds, rain, hailstorms; but a well-designed building, if it is to be a virtuous structure, can also display motion just by its negativity. If you recall your physics you'll remember that there is as much energy in reaction as there is in action."

"I don't remember too much physics, Peter. Just a little Trowbridge. 'To be a virtuous structure . . .' isn't that what you said?"

"Is that what I said?"

"Don't be coy."

"What will you be doing in Nice?"

"You're changing the subject."

"I'm changing the subject."

"The same as I was doing at Wolf Ranch. Scouting locations."

Ibsen reached under the seat and pulled out an attaché

case. She opened it and removed a script.

"This is the screenplay based on a novel by Walter Orenn. It is called *Weekend*. Have you read the book?"

"No. Should I have?"

"No."

"Bad?"

"No. Slick. It will make a good commercial movie. It's sort of fun."

Ibsen reached into her purse and brought out a diminutive pair of horn-rimmed glasses. She wiped the lenses with the edges of her scarf and put them on.

"Didn't know I wore glasses, did you?"

"I've never seen them on you."

"I wore contact lenses the other day, you didn't know that either."

"I was too busy watching other things. You look marvelous in glasses."

"Everyone says that. I don't know how to feel about that. Do I have sort of a vacuous look without them?"

"Do you wear them when you make love?"

"What kind of question is that?"

"It is a perfectly good question."

"I never have, but I'd be happy to oblige."

"I am trying to answer for myself why I like you with glasses."

"I am waiting."

"I think, really, Ibsen, your features are so perfect, that the glasses give you a little vulnerability."

"That sounds like a hell of a nice compliment."

"Well, good."

Ibsen looked at me quite intently then kissed me fully on the lips. "You are the most guileless man I've ever known."

"Weekend!"

"All right, Weekend. Oh hell, Peter. I'm not going to read the whole thing. It's a contemporary love story. I need a yacht, a train station, a chic bar, a hotel, a church . . ."

"That doesn't sound too difficult."

"It's not. I just have to decide which yacht would look good on Paul Newman, which depot would bring tears to Catherine Deneuve."

"Wouldn't it be lovely if all architecture were set designing? If we could only build for beauty and then tear down the structures when they annoy us?"

"Not everyone is as ruthlessly aesthetic as you."

"Perhaps that's true, Ibsen, but it is incumbent on architects to give some beauty to our fellow man. We should stimulate, encourage, we should lead the way."

"If you don't take your hand away from where you have it, you're going to stimulate me right on top of you."

I pulled the small wool blanket over us, bunched up the inadequate little pillows under my head and drew Ibsen even closer to me. We talked for hours, like children after the lights had been put out, and finally Ibsen fell asleep. I looked at her face, it was a warm strong, young face, in total repose, quite peaceful and very beautiful. I admired her courage, her independence, her trust, shuffling between continents like an airborne gypsy, and finally I too became drowsy, massaged by the staccato vibrations of the aircraft, knowing that six inches from my head existed a hostile atmosphere, subzero temperatures, howling winds. I looked at my watch. We were crossing the Pole.

We arrived in Copenhagen the following evening. It was cool and there was a light rain, but the fresh air felt good and clean after all the hours in the cabin of the aircraft. We passed through customs, hailed a cab. It was eleven o'clock when we arrived at the D'Angleterre; the spacious marble-floored lobby was almost deserted, a desk clerk dressed in a shabby cutaway welcomed us and an old bellhop showed us to our room, equally cavernous, chilly.

"I'll use the bathroom," Ibsen said, and I changed into a new pair of pajamas. They were light blue and had white piping about the collar and lapels. I looked at myself in the mirror, at my unshaven face, my bloodshot sleep-poor eyes and dove under the great eiderdown comforter on our bed. I turned off the light and watched Ibsen open the door to the bathroom, her naked figure silhouetted clearly under a shorty nightgown, all gauze and lace.

She shut off the light and joined me in bed. We kissed and I could smell the soap she had used on her face. It was an odor I remembered from my childhood in Germany. We fell asleep.

10

I AWOKE before Ibsen. It was early morning and a gray-blue light filtered through the drapes. I rose and sat on a window ledge, pulled aside the delicate lace-bordered curtain, and watched Copenhagen below me, rested, fresh and precise. Our room faced the square in front of the hotel and the yellow trams, festooned with colorful graphics, were making graceful arcs, stopping directly opposite me to discharge early morning workers. Hundreds of bicycles and motorscooters swarmed in from sidestreets like migrating birds en route, their riders purposeful and unruffled, dressed for their daily functions. Shopkeepers were sweeping the sidewalks in front of their establishments. Men were washing windows and polishing brass plaques. Delivery trucks stopped and drivers unloaded crates and barrels onto sidewalk elevators which disappeared below the level of the street. Gardeners were trimming neat hedges of the small park in the center of the square, weeding the flower beds of petunias and asters. A few soldiers in dress uniform stood in front of the hotel; young boys in short pants and colorful blazers were heading for school in clusters of three or four, their books, strapped together by leather belts, swinging over their shoulders.

❧

I WAS ten years old and a Quintaner in the Kaiser Wilhelm Gymnasium when Hitlerism became a threat. It was a fifteen-minute walk from my house to the school and I had done it for three years with the same group of boys. We would stop occasionally at the butcher shop and buy fresh blood sausage, still warm and fragrant, dawdle at the little stationery store with its smell of graphite and admire four-color fountain pens, notebooks with celluloid covers, but of late, we would pause to read *The Volkischer Beobachter* displayed at the bus stop in a crude wooden frame covered with wire mesh. There were frightening headlines and monstrous caricatures invariably showing a Jew with a gargantuan, hairy levantine nose drooling over a pure, blond Aryan girl.

Not having been raised religiously, but rather coming from a home life filled with Streseman's liberalism, where emphasis was on Germanicism, not Judaism, I felt dissociated, almost mildly titillated by these daily horror stories. It was not until months later that several older boys took my bicycle. It had been new that Christmas, with chrome fenders and a speedometer and a bell which rang if one pulled a leather strap on the handlebar to allow it to make contact with the rotating front wheel.

There were three boys, no more than a year older than myself. I knew their names and where they lived and they simply demanded my bicycle. I tried to ride away but they put a stick between the spokes. They called me a rich, no-good Jew, other things I can't recall.

I ran home and told my father. I told him who had taken my bicycle and where they lived and he threw up his hands. I begged him to call the police and he told me to forget the bicycle, to forget what happened. It was the last day I would attend school. It was the last day I left our house without an adult accompanying me.

My father had phoned the gymnasium and spoken to the headmaster. He understood, and wished me well. He spoke to me personally. There were tears in my eyes when I hung up the receiver. I was learning what it meant to be a Jew.

But looking at the square in Copenhagen below me brought more than sad memories. The very shape of the trams pulling unmotorized cars, the sight of a vendor carrying a sack full of soft pretzels, a woman pushing a perambulator, large, clumsy and hooded like a rickshaw, replowed furrows of my memories which had lain fallow for years. Suddenly I thought of the green verdant meadows of Koenigstein and the old castle I had explored as a child, climbing into each parapet, holding off enemy after enemy with my cork-stoppered cannon. The seemingly endless walks on tiny paths worn into the tall grass to reach a swimming tank, the ambrosia of young apple cider in the early days of fall, the taste of freshly made mustard, of new potatoes with dill sauce, of sledding down a modest incline in the first snows of January. I felt the fallacy that children are adaptable. I, too, had been a refugee, and though I may have learned to speak English flawlessly in just a few months and mastered the nuances of hopscotch and pitching pennies, the guts of my childhood had also been ripped open: there were new smells to replace the old, new sights, new sounds, new textures, new new, new, and strange.

✦

I LET GO the drapes and looked at Ibsen, her face buried in one arm, her shoulder and one breast naked above the sheet. She had never displayed any shyness these few days I had known her and never made me feel that she was gifting me with her nakedness, and I finally could not contain myself any longer. I threw myself on the bed, kissing her breast, practically devouring it with my mouth, and Ibsen instinctively turned toward me, slowly awakening, her nipple growing hard between my lips, and then I kissed her neck and her ear and ran my mouth down the small of her back, turning her, kissing her stomach, her thighs, burrowing myself between her legs and finally Ibsen lay back, her head on the pillow, her eyes open and on the ceiling.

"More, Peter," she said, "more darling, more," and her viscous wetness covered my face and her stomach and the inside of her thighs until I could feel every nerve in her body respond to my tongue, feel climax after climax as my hands held her little buttocks, until one stroke down her lovely straight spine could set up one more paroxysm and her breasts pushed against my chest and my stomach and my

100

hand could hold the nape of her slender neck now moist also from fine perspiration at the root of her hair, and all of her was one with me, her arms and legs and her torso and her face, her beautiful lips, open, her eyes, now open now closed, her nose, her cheekbones, her chin, the cleft between her breasts and the feel of one foot in my hand as I pushed back her legs once more, once more.

We made love for maybe an hour, maybe two, I don't remember. One passion fed on another until I finally collapsed next to her, visibly shaken, trying to light a cigarette, trying to relate my body to the edge of the bed, the floor of the room, the ceiling, the window morning-bright to my left.

"Where did you learn how to make love like that Peter?"

"I've never made love like that."

Ibsen said nothing and conformed her naked body to my back, circling my stomach with her arms.

"You don't believe that, do you?"

"I do believe you, darling. Did it bother you?"

"I've never felt so close to anyone Ibsen. I am, I am . . ." I hesitated and turned to face her, "I didn't know I *could* make love like that," and then I buried my head in her breasts and fell asleep.

I slept a delicious drugged sleep, and finally awoke and saw Ibsen, dressed in a tiny tweed skirt and a well-pressed white linen blouse, sitting at the edge of my bed.

"Well, Mr. Trowbridge."

"Well, what?"

"Just because you've had a little passion in your life, doesn't mean you can sleep the whole morning away."

"And why not? Where is the night nurse? I want the night nurse back. She's got the smallest, softest, warmest fanny."

"The night nurse, Mr. Trowbridge, has gone home. She has washed her sins away in a tingling hot shower, with pine-needle soap and a very rough washcloth."

"I see."

"I am Miss Swenson from the Danish Tourist Bureau."

"What kind of fanny do you have?"

"Never mind my fanny, Mr. Trowbridge. There is much to do, much to see. We're a half hour late to Hamlet's Castle already."

"The night nurse had the same color hair as you."

"Really."

"Except it wasn't tightly bound the way you wear it with a ribbon."

"A black velvet ribbon."

"Her hair was all over her face, with abandon. A little moist, I remember."

"Abandon. I see. Now, Mr. Trowbridge, I have some fresh Danish. In Finland, you get fresh Finnish. And here is hot steaming coffee and a little present."

"For me?"

"For you, Mr. Trowbridge. Welcome to Denmark."

It was a small package, wrapped in black tissue paper, a chaste gold ribbon, a small seal in one corner. I opened it carefully and discovered an exquisite rosewood cigarette box, with inlaid silver squares on its cover.

"It's beautiful Ibsen. What did I do to deserve this?"

"You're a nice man."

I kissed her.

"You need a shave."

I felt my chin.

"I thought I'd grow a beard."

"I wonder how you'd look with a beard."

"Like a scrawny Hemingway. Come on. Out of my way. The way you cross your legs, you'll be back in this bed in no time."

We walked through downtown Copenhagen savoring through the windows the teak and silver, the glassware and embroidery; had lunch of tiny sandwiches and aquavit at the Royal Danish Yacht Club where I had guest privileges, watched the fishermen come in with the day's catch and finally ended up dining in a tiny, elegant candlelit restaurant in Tivoli, drinking more aquavit, more draft beer and amusing ourselves making fun of the American tourists who bordered our table.

"They are not from Texas," Ibsen insisted. "They're from Arizona."

"Texas."

"You see that great swash of batiste covering that woman's bosom? That is right off the rack at Goldwaters. Neiman Marcus wouldn't carry such a thing."

"She bought it at Macy's in New York, dummy, when father got the red vest."

"I like the red vest. It goes with his green mohair shirt. I love that luminescent fabric."

"He actually looks like a traffic signal."

"Maybe he is a traffic signal."

"He's signaling the waitress."

"I knew it, see I knew it, Peter. He wants some catsup."

"Well, why don't they give him some catsup?"

"They've been perfecting the sauces in this restaurant for two hundred and fifty years."

"You're so cruel, Ibsen. If the poor man wants catsup, he should have it. He'd much rather be back in Dallas anyway."

"Tucson."

"Dallas. Only came because his wife forced him to come."

"Poor man."

"Got caught one night with the manicurist from the Elks Club. Just couldn't help himself the way she rubbed the hand lotion into the palm of his hand when she finished with his cuticles. Sort of pulling the hand to her bosom as a finale."

"What is it about manicurists?"

"The fingers are the only part of a man's anatomy which may be legally manipulated by the opposite sex."

"Don't they have lady dentists, or . . . ?"

"Or what?"

"It wasn't nice what I was thinking."

"We've got to be nice."

"I thought he might be a dentist."

"Why don't we ask him?"

"He's probably head librarian at the Brookings Institute."

"Maybe he's on his way to get the Nobel Prize. Just stopped off for a little catsup in Denmark."

"Correct."

"They'd be real pleased to talk to some folks from back home, Ibsen."

"You'd probably forget my name when we'd get around to the introductions."

"Probably."

"And I'm sure they're going to Nice, just like we are."

"Bully."

"And we'd forever be running into them. I bet he wears those overlong plaid Bermuda shorts."

"And black knee-length socks and black shoes."

"And real icky white legs."

"I knew it, I knew it Ibsen."

"What, what?"

"I knew he would have a plastic pocket liner on his shirt pocket."

"My God, what are all those things he's got sticking in there?"

"A lifetime ball-point pen."

"Yes?"

"A tire pressure gauge."

"Yes."

"A combination Phillips Screwdriver and nail clippers. A penlight."

"Of course."

"And a thermometer."

"Rectal or oral?"

"Ibsen Iazzo!"

"You *do* know my name."

"More aquavit?"

"More aquavit. More aquavit. No. No more aquavit. Pay up. Let's get out of here. I need some air. Some exercise."

We walked the empty streets of Copenhagen, stopping occasionally to peer into the small provocative windows of a silversmith, but all the aquavit had not worn off. Returning to the hotel, I phoned room service and asked them to wake us at six. We collapsed into bed managing only to kiss each other good night before falling asleep.

11

NICE was still balmy when we arrived at Pension Aida at ten in the evening. A bubbling, dark-haired female concierge who knew Ibsen from previous visits showed us our quarters and helped with the luggage. It was a lovely room, with a high ceiling and three high clerestory windows, heavily draped in velvet facing the veranda. It was all typically French, the grandeur of the furnishings clashing with the primitiveness of the plumbing, the materials rich but faded and shopworn. A bowl of cut flowers sat on the dresser, marigolds, cornflowers, lilacs, mums, and Ibsen instinctively rearranged them, pulling up one flower, breaking off the stem of another and replacing it.

"There. I think I'll take a bath. You should see the bathtub. I think it's Napoleonic."

I opened the door to the veranda and stepped out. It was still such a beautiful warm night; the sounds of Nice, the smell of mimosa and lilac, and the splashing of Ibsen prattling about the tub.

I hesitated momentarily, then entered the archaic bathroom. Ibsen looked truly beautiful, only her toes and the nipples of her breasts were visible above the suds-filled water.

"Don't just stand there, make yourself useful: scrub my back."

I did, and then I left as suddenly as I had appeared and returned to the porch. A few minutes later Ibsen joined me, a bath towel wrapped around her, another one over her hair. She put her arms about my waist and I could feel her warmth yet her dampness and the smell of some wild and erotic perfume.

"Why did you leave so suddenly Peter?"

"Because I'm being foolish."

"How?"

"The kid in the candy factory."

"Are you afraid you'll tire of me?"

"That's the last thing I'm afraid of, it's just the opposite."

"It's only our second day, Peter."

"When you suggested this safari, my love, I knew I couldn't say goodbye. What makes you think I can manfully shake your hand when *this* week is over?"

"Let's have our week first, darling. I want to take a walk to the harbor and see whether the Kahn yacht is at its dock. I'd love to use it for the movie. You should see it anyway."

"Who is Kahn?"

"An independent producer. He lives on his boat. Works on it. Neat. What's it like to be really rich, Peter?"

"I wouldn't know."

"You said you had over a million dollars. I'd say that was really rich."

"There is a million dollars in trusts, and stocks and bonds. I've never seen it all in one pile. Mary's family has an attorney. He handles all of it."

"I didn't mean you had it all in one pile in front of you. What I am wondering is whether it gives you great freedom?"

"It could, I suppose Ibsen, but Mary's family just simply isn't constituted that way. There is a life style, certainly. Full-time help and a gardener in the country, and a laundress and the children get their teeth straightened and go to a good summer camp. I suppose if you had none of these things they would sound luxurious. But there is nothing done impetuously. My house is on a side street in Pacific Heights. It has no view of the bay. We purchased it about a year after we were married. Mary's father thought it was a sensible investment. I hate the damned place. What's the point of living in that city if you can't see the bay. Even *you* have a great view."

"Why don't you build a house?"

"Why didn't I? I know it all sounds insane, darling. It *is* insane. There is a frugality in Mary's family. A house is to keep you warm, to give each child a bedroom, to allow you enough room to seat twelve people in the dining room. A house is bought with an eye toward resale. 'Soon the children will be grown,' the war cry goes. 'Then we can move to an apartment.' Life is not a joy. Life is not an adventure. It is something you *endure,* by God. Who said it should be free, or beautiful or exciting. You exist to allow your children to exist the way you did. You are a link, not the beginning, not the end. A link in an endless chain of placid, drab, unruffled security. No chances, no gambles, no spirit."

"You built a showplace in Atherton. I've seen it often in the Journals."

"It is a lovely house. We use it for three months during the summer. September thirtieth the carpeting is rolled up. The furniture is covered. The water is drained from the pool. The only joy I've ever derived from it was building it."

"I don't mean to pry, Peter."

"Pry all you want."

"If you don't like the way you live, why do it?"

"I was a refugee boy. Remember? When I graduated from Taliesen West, I had every intention to go in with Wang, Shiller & Prothro, but Mary's father offered me a job in his firm. Designing warehouses, loading docks, store fixtures. It paid twenty-five thousand dollars a year. That was an awful lot of money for a kid who never had any. I sold out. What the hell. Why deny it? It took me five years to join my friends, and only on a consulting basis. I still work for Danner part of the time."

Ibsen put her arm in mine and steered me toward the door.

"To the Kahn yacht."

"The Kahn yacht, come on, that sounds absolutely ridiculous."

"Why. What sounds better, the Morgan yacht—the Kennedy yacht?"

"Yes, that sounds better."

"You German Jews are all antisemites."

"True, true. If Hitler would only have allowed it, we would have made marvelous Nazis."

"I can well imagine."

Ibsen had changed into a light-blue chiffon dress. She looked really quite pristine and vibrant. Her hair loose, framing her face with each turn of her head and each movement of her body creating a new picture. We walked down Carabecel to the Place Jean Moulin still filled with children playing hide and seek in the waning light of day. We circled the Musée d'histoire naturelle, past Place Garibaldi and took Rue Cassini to the port.

It was a small harbor bordered by commercial structures and filled for the most part with fishing vessels. Somehow the yachts, mostly large sailboats, looked very pristine and out of place like children wearing their Sunday best to a hay ride. The Kahn yacht, as Ibsen pointed her out, was moored close to the mouth of the harbor, a magnificent motor-sailer, well over a hundred feet in length, extravagantly lit, the almost obscene illuminations mirrored in the blackness of the Mediterranean.

Ibsen guided me along the maze of docks, until we reached a small, gated landing. A sign over the gate read VALKYRIE and we rang a ship's bell to summon a young boy behind the wheel of a well-varnished speed boat. She spoke to him in French, he helped us on board, cast off the dock-frayed lines and headed into the harbor with much gusto, betraying his youth more than his seamanship. The wind felt warm and moist and I watched it mold Ibsen's flimsy dress to her body. The shore line came into perspective, the great hotels along the Promenade des Anglais strung out like so many diamonds in a diadem of lesser jewels.

I held Ibsen's hand and wished the boy and the speed-boat would keep their course, past the Kahn yacht, the breakwater, out into open waters, Africa, I didn't care, but we approached the *Valkyrie* with an elegant turn to star-board the boy cutting his speed more with his rudder than his engine, tying his craft to the boarding ladder of the mother ship.

We jumped from boat to ladder and ascended it pre-cariously to the welcoming shouts of the assembled above us. There were eight people in our welcoming party, all of them middle-aged, the men wearing white ducks and sport shirts, the women dressed in simple shifts; all of them brown, salt-burned, a little brittle, a little dry.

Everyone knew Ibsen and were obviously delighted to see her; there was much embracing and kissing.

"Mr. Kahn, Peter Trowbridge."

"The architect?"

"The very one."

"I'm honored."

"Mr. Casuela, Mr. Wells, Mrs. Wells, Mary Farnum, Mr. Elbertson, my mother, Mrs. Kahn, Richard Wohter."

We shook hands and Alfred Kahn shepherded us leisurely to the fantail, where remnants of a sumptuous buffet were still in evidence—halves of ornamental aspics, platters of sausage and cheese garnished with mint leaves and parsley, silver serving dishes heated by small cans of Sterno.

Kahn had not released Ibsen since he embraced her on

our arrival and as he guided her to a seat beside his own, the rest of us seated ourselves in great white wicker chairs, all of it very reminiscent of Commodore Lipton on a calm day in Chesapeake Bay.

"I heard you were coming," Kahn said, "but I didn't know when. I would have had fireworks, floral displays, native divers."

"At least, Albert. How *did* you know I was coming?"

"Albert Kahn knows all, sees all."

"Really, darling, how? I hadn't decided till the last minute to head in this direction."

"I had a wire from a friend of yours in Washington, D.C."

"John Perry?"

"The very one."

"What did he want?"

"I'll let you see the wire."

Ibsen sensed my confusion and stated, somewhat needlessly, "I haven't seen him in over a year," and Kahn, realizing that he had perhaps betrayed something he should have told Ibsen privately, made haste to change the subject.

"You'll have to forgive us, Mr. Trowbridge, but since we are in the movie business, we seem always to be talking about the movie business."

"Go right ahead."

"What I was saying was that I think I am finally going to get my just punishment."

"You haven't done anything wrong, Albert," his mother chided, and everyone laughed.

"You see, it pays to have one's mother along, but seriously, what we were saying, Ibsen, is that most of us, Bill, Walter, myself," he pointed about the assembled, "came here to Italy, some to Yugoslavia, to Spain, found ourselves some run-down American gorilla and shot low-budget pictures. The local women were expendable, the extras came for nothing, the sets were free."

"I wish you'd get Jimmy Stewart in a picture, Alfred," his mother said. "He seems like such a nice man."

"He'll be working in Europe soon, the way he's selling tickets. No, the point of my story is that we are in the midst of a revolution. *Kids* are shooting movies, Fonda, Dennis Hopper, Dustin Hoffman. Movies for three or four hundred thousand that are *grossing*. Why? What kind of stories? *Easy Rider. Midnight Cowboy.* I've never seen such scripts. What's it all about, Ibsen?"

"Relevance."

"What relevance? A couple kids filled with cocaine, riding around America on a motorcycle is relevance?"

"It's relevance to the kids. They're the ones that buy the tickets. Ten guys using one apartment during working hours? Is that relevant? Two divorced idiots living together? That's relevant? Come on."

"That has universality. Everyone can identify."

"Everyone but theatergoers."

Kahn patted Ibsen's knee.

"She's right," he said. "She's right. Here I am, stuck on this tub in the Mediterranean."

"Why do you have to live on a boat?" Kahn's mother asked, but he ignored her.

"Stuck in Nice, watching the movie business go to hell. What brings *you* here, Ibsen?"

"I came primarily to find out *why* you have to live on a boat."

"Oh, Sweetheart, you are too pretty to be that smart."

We were drinking a very dry champagne and my glass seemed to be refilled by elfins. Several mess-coated waiters floated about our group, lighting cigarettes, cleaning ash trays, offering mints, water, fruit.

"You should really marry me, Ibsen. What sort of sets are you going to design when the script calls for a motorcycle and the Arizona desert?"

"I'm glad you mentioned sets. I need the *Valkyrie* for a week's shooting"

"What picture? *Weekend?*"

"The very one."

"You could do it in a studio."

"We could, but why?"

"What would I do for a week? I get seasick on land."

"You can join us," one of the other women said. "We're going on a safari."

"Not for me, Ethel. I shot a Tarzan picture in Somaliland a few years ago. Never again."

"We will discuss?" Ibsen said pertly, now patting Kahn's knee.

"We will discuss. What great commission brings you to Nice, Mr. Trowbridge?"

"No commission."

"A holiday?"

"I am here because Ibsen is here." There was a momentary silence and I did not look at Ibsen after making the statement. I could not even explain this forthrightness, but Kahn finally broke the silence.

"I could not find a better reason myself."

We walked arm in arm through the narrow streets of Nice after leaving the *Valkyrie*. It was still warm even past midnight, but the town did not want to relinquish the day either. Shops were open and the eternal tourist still haggled with the merchants. The sidewalk cafés were crowded, a good many American students, many of them bearded, wearing leather jackets and jeans, their girls in faded denim shirts open to their navels. Uniformed doormen were still wheeling Rolls-Royces up the driveways of the Palace and the Grand Hotels, engulfing powdered, gray-haired ladies, their necks bound in strands of pearls, their poodles profusely beribboned.

We found a corner at La Piques, ordered a bottle of red wine and played with the softened edges of a large red candle burning in the middle of our small round table.

"You're very quiet Peter. Is something wrong?"

I shook my head. "No. Nothing is wrong."

"What is it then?"

"I don't know why I should presume to know you as I thought I knew you. All I am at this stage no doubt is the world's greatest authority on your navel."

"You hold a record for my fanny, too."

"Indeed, but I realized tonight that we are really still strangers."

"Did something offend you on Kahn's boat?"

"Not in the least. Perhaps I was a little disappointed."

"What did you expect? Isn't it a magnificent boat?"

"The boat is exquisite. I toured it from stem to stern with Kahn. He is very proud of it."

"Then what?"

"Well, there it sits, this jewel, this set if you will, a white yacht in the midnight ocean of Nice. A warm, windless star-filled night. A yacht filled with aging paunchy merchants whose business happens to be movies, discussing their wares."

Ibsen smiled. "Where were the starlets? The phony counts? The real ones? The alcoholics, the fifteen-year-old Eurasian girls?"

"Yes, where were they?"

"They're here, they're around, on other yachts in other clubs. . . . Alfred Kahn, despite his self-deprecation, is one of the biggest men in the business. He's been on the Riviera a long time. He can afford the luxury of decent, ordinary friends."

"I appreciated that Ibsen, but where do you fit in?"

"Why? Do you believe I belong with all the swingers?"

"No, darling, not all, but you are so young. So very young. I can't really believe you belong anywhere yet."

"I'm twenty-six. I am a set designer, remember? The studio counts on me. I need men like Albert Kahn. I'll get the *Valkyrie* for a week."

"I know," I said.

But how, I wondered, but I didn't ask.

12

I AWOKE the following morning to find Ibsen gone from bed, but could see her foot through the veranda door. I rose and saw her lying on the floor of the patio. She had spread a beach towel on the tiles and she was very still and very naked. A series of drawings were scattered near her hand, a half-drunk glass of orange juice, an empty cup of coffee.

I stood at the veranda door looking at Ibsen and beyond. Below us were the houses cascading in their whiteness and linearity like a random set of dominoes. They were simple stone structures, whitewashed, the deep-set windows, bleak and lifeless; only the ever-present flower boxes filled with well-tended blood-red geraniums gave a measure of love to the scene. Below it all lay the Mediterranean, dark-blue and calm, fusing into an equally blue horizon. I could smell pepper and oleander and mustard, and yet I heard no sounds.

Ibsen was so totally naked, the areolas about her nipples

a very light pink, her pubic hair sparse and straw colored, the fine blond hair on her arms and legs almost invisible in the sunlight. She aroused more admiration than sensuality in this state, but once I kissed her, watched her rise, seeing her breasts, which had practically lost all dimension when she lay on her back, assume their fullness when she sat on her feet and brazenly exposed her vagina, the inner man so easily gave way to the animal.

Unwashed and unshaven, my mouth still tasting of garlic and the sediments of dry red wine from the night before, I made love. I was unconcerned about the possibility of prying eyes, of neighboring villas or the sudden entry of a parlormaid. It was the warm sunlight, the stillness of the air, the pungent aromas, the grace of a stand of bougainvillea climbing one wall of our patio, its delicate petals and defiant pinkish redness, their convolutions and rhythm not unlike Ibsen entwined in me.

We made love playfully, teasing, giving, taking, almost at times a pastiche; Ibsen's face intent then Chaplinesque, saying, "Yes, Peter, that's it, don't give a damn," at other times, "Please darling oh God, that's so good, no, stop, once more, please, Peter. I love you, I love you. I love you. Don't leave. Don't stop, don't go away. Darling. Darling. You like that? I can't stop. You like it? Why should I stop? Come on? Be hedonistic, Peter. Oh, goddamn, Peter. Peter. Peter?"

I had finally landed on the tile floor of the patio and felt the warmth of its glaze tingling my skin. I rolled over and looked at Ibsen's drawings for the sets of *Weekend*. She drew well and cleanly but there was something pedestrian about her approach.

"Do you mind if I make some changes?"

"I wish you would." Ibsen handed me a drafting pencil and I began to modify the interior of the waterfront café, a railway station, an abandoned church in the foothills above Nice, and finally I discarded the altered drawings and spread fresh paper in front of me and drew structures anew, no longer bound by the outlines of Ibsen's work. I found myself lecturing, almost unconsciously, not worrying whether I sounded fatuous at all.

"You must remember the height of the occupants, darling. Anthropomorphy is the keystone to human architecture. You see this window, this roof line? It is too high. Twelve feet, fourteen feet at best in a room twenty by thirty. This is all you need to depict grandeur for a six-foot man. You cannot ignore endless square footage of unused air space. It is hard to heat, hard to live with."

"What are these?"

"Rafters."

"I know they're rafters. Do you establish this king post here and here?"

"Yes."

"Yes?" Ibsen was still on the deck chair, her head propped by her elbow.

"How dull," I said. "All you kids were ruined by Mies. That fucking dry Hun. Less is more. What the hell does *that* mean? Less is more. Less is *less*. A circle is more noble than a straight line, an oval is more noble than a circle.

Symmetrical ellipticism is divine and nothing is more sacred than a parabola.

"Look here," I said somewhat sternly. "You can vault this ceiling," and I did so with my pencil, "or you can mansard it or you can combine the two or you can spire it or you can striate it, the way the Byzantines did it.

"Every generation finds some messiah. Good old Mies van der Rohe and his goddammed Bauhaus. A whole religion based on the theory that workmen can only exist with a level.

"Do you ever see a carpenter with a French curve in his tool kit? Or an architect for that matter?

"There, *this* is a railway station. It is a structure of anticipation. The arrival of a great puffing steel monster, the departure of a great puffing monster. It should be warm and exciting, it is the point of contact between flesh and blood and big heaving inhuman machines. Scale it down, scale it down. This is where the train arrives, the phallus entering the vagina. *Here* is where the passengers cluster, warmth, warmth, flowerpots, magazines, luggage carts, posters, signs, a flower stand, a vendor selling pillows, blankets, a Salvation Army troupe, a soldier of God beating the bass drum, women with tambourines, a lady with a trumpet—children, lots of children, clutching the skirts of their mothers, teddy bears, and puffing steam everywhere like patches of fog on a dawn-filled lake, grease cans and flares and signal lanterns, markers, switch lights, people kissing, people crying, kerchiefs, bandanas, packages of food, mugs of coffee and skins of wine, and mystery much mystery, signs which mean nothing—D-G 1811, COUPLE ON RAMP, UNSTEADY, TURN LEFT —women in saris, clerics in floor-length tunics holding polished leather briefcases."

I threw down the pencil and turned away from the drawing.

Ibsen looked at me quietly for a minute, as if seeing me for the first time, then threw her arms around my neck. She was almost crying.

"Why, Peter Trowbridge, why are you designing warehouses? Why are you half-time partner in that dumb alliance you have, why, why are you trading your gift for a house in the country, a man who washes windows twice a month, a wife who doesn't make you happy, a cockteasing bloodless mistress?"

"Motus animi continous, to quote Cellini, motus animi continous, this is where eloquence resides."

"Bullshit Peter. I'll respect your assessment of Mies, but don't counter Cellini. He was equally passionless. Brutal, clean, industrious, logical, writhing life out of mathematics, out of reason, out of logic, but it can't be done."

I had never seen Ibsen quite so animated. No longer was I aware of her nakedness (or my own for that matter). I watched her face and the intensity of her eyes, the movement of her hands.

"I know all about the insecurity of the refugee boy, the desire for security, the drive for the orderly life, but you're not unique, darling. My father bolted when I was a child. We lived by my mother's wits. Sure she was an educated woman, she had a salable commodity, but she was still only a lonely professor of philosophy, our livelihood depended on the whims of boards of regents, of faculty committees, our daily bread hung on the balance of her expressions of very radical theories of human existence and intellectually painful allowances for pedantry.

"I traveled from Antioch to Foxcroft, from Holyoke to Sarah Lawrence, from Bryn Mawr to Vassar to Wellesley. Not with matching sets of luggage containing new bedspreads, new drapes, new clothes, not with bubbling cloying relatives on days of academic festivities. No sir. Like an army brat, in a series of run-down faculty residences, with run-down yards and careless maintenance. My closets were not filled with frilly dresses and cuddly cashmeres. My Christmases consisted of volumes of Rilke and Shelley and the shorter works of Schiller. My off hours were spent being quiet while my mother wrote endless, endless papers, publishing, publishing time after time to stay afloat in academe.

"No junior proms, no football games, no beer nights on Fraternity Row. Work. What is it you said, 'Motus animus continous.' You bet. School work and part-time work. The college cafeteria, the college library, the college laundry, the college bookshop . . . to hell with it darling. Go out and buy some baguettes and some pâté and pickles and a very expensive bottle of wine."

I spent the remainder of the morning in the open stalls of Caramacel, watching elegant French women meticulously dressed in well-cut linen suits expertly pick their daily needs. They fondled the endive and the watercress, turned each potato as if it were a diamond and perhaps flawed. They bought fruit and vegetables, breads, meat, poultry all with the same meticulousness; flowers from a small stand, cornflowers, marigolds, asters, stowing each item carefully into little net nylon sacks, remaining through all the haggling, the pushing and fondling still elegant, unruffled and seemingly quite ready for an unholy alliance before noon.

I, too, stopped, picking items really more for color and shape than taste and returned home to find Ibsen highly amused with my choice.

"Are you going to make a mobile with this or am I supposed to whip up a meal? This avocado will not ripen for at least two weeks. This meat needs to be marinated, this cheese is only good when it runs away from you."

"Improvise, my love; improvise. There are mushrooms, dills, leek, onions, goose eggs, chives, radishes, pâté, for a veritable cornucopia of southern France."

"Go read a book," she said, shoving me toward the patio, "play with yourself. I don't know why I ever let you go shopping."

As Cahill, Thomas, Wang and Trowbridge grew over the years, we had taken a succession of young architects into the firm, young men picked more for their promise than their portfolios, and though I was rarely envious of their particular talents, I coveted their life style. This was the generation unfettered by memories of the Great Depression, not bothered by security, by convention, and though they all treated me with great deference, I knew a wall existed which I could not scale and they were anxious to retain intact.

They were married, most of them, to young pert vibrant girls in some way reminding me of Ibsen, and I would watch them draw their check at week's end, heading for the snow, for the beaches, great healthy divertissements which would no doubt end in bed, and I spent endless evenings at vacuous dinner parties thinking of their naked sunburned bodies in the most erotic of positions.

It was true, I could go through the drafting room with great authority and I could find numerous solutions to problems which seemed unsolvable to the apprentices on paper. I had the experience and the imagination. I had for better or worse a true love for my profession, and yet I found myself time after time looking at one of my admiring apprentices after I had redrawn a profile or changed a roof line, wanting to say, "Now teach me. Teach me about this dumb life. Teach me about this dumb happiness that plays on your face as you walk out of here at five o'clock tonight. Am I so old? So dull? I am forty-two," I wanted to scream. "Forty-two? Do you think I live only to work? Do you think all my juices are dried up?"

"I call this dish the Riviera Surprise," Ibsen announced, bringing forth two steaming plates. "It contains everything from anchovies to heartburn and you may have some delicious coconut syrup to top it off."

"I'll open the coconut," I said and tasted the concoction. "It's really very good."

"Of course it's really very good. I used one half a bottle of wine. Imagine getting a hangover from a goulash . . ."

"Do you think we could rent a sailboat, Ibsen?"

"Why not? The entire Riviera is for rent."

"I have been studying the charts in Michelin, and deduced that it is about a 12-kilometer run to Cap Ferrat. If I can obtain a vessel and you provision it (since you have so little faith in my procurements), we should depart in two hours and make port by sundown."

"It sounds divine Peter, but I warn you, I am not much help in a boat."

"You can act as a masthead, stripped to the waist."

"I'm very good at that."

"I know." I pulled her close to me and buried my head in her stomach, kissing her navel which felt warm and soft and smelled of olive oil.

"You'd better stop doing that if you want to set sail today."

There was a knock on the door; I rose. It was the concierge, who handed me a telegram. It was for Ibsen.

She opened it, read it, said nothing and replaced it in the envelope, looking somewhat studiedly at the sea below us.

"John Perry?" I asked.

"How did you know?"

"Kahn mentioned a wire from him last night."

"That's right, I forgot."

"Do you want to talk about it?"

"There is nothing to talk about Peter."

"Old boyfriend?"

She nodded her head, tapping her leg with the telegram, then tearing it up, letting the pieces fly down the terrace.

"It's nothing, Peter. John Perry is a son of a bitch."

"On that note," I said, "let us continue with our merriment."

"Really darling," Ibsen said, "don't read anything into my behavior. I'll tell you about John sometime. Not now."

We packed a few belongings into a small bag; sweaters, underwear, toilet articles, Bermudas, bathing suits, a bottle of brandy, and headed for the port, parting at Place Guynemer.

"I'll see you on the docks, darling. Don't let those Frenchmen take all your money."

There were numerous yachts available for charter and I finally picked a thirty-foot wooden sloop owned by a Scotsman.

"She's not a young boat," he said, "but she's quite fast. Built by Farrow and Dunning in Glasgow in 1934. She's got Dacron sails, roller reefing, but you won't be needing it this time of year. Where are you planning to go?"

"Cap Ferrat."

"Aah, that's a lovely sail. Just point southeast. It's a beam reach all the way."

I stepped on board and took the halyards off the cleats, spread the hemp apart at its fold to test its vitality. I checked the play in the rudder, the tuning of the stays, opened the bilges and ran my hand along the seams of the fuel tank to check for leaks.

"You seem to know what it's about," the Scotsman said. "Some of these fellows rent a boat, can't tell port from starboard."

The cabin was comfortable with ample head room. Two

bunks, one on each side, a small galley aft near the ladder to the cockpit, a head and sail locker forward. An open skylight gave air and warmth to the interior.

"Will you be single-handing her?"

"Almost," I said. "Although I'll have a deckhand."

"She sails like a lady," he said, "but there's lots of winches aboard if you need them."

I paid my deposit and started to ready the boat for our trip, removing the sail covers, the scissors which held the main boom, then tied on the genoa jib. I started the engine, checked the exhaust, placed cushions on the teak cockpit seats and helped Ibsen on board, carrying two armloads of supplies.

"What a beautiful boat. What is her name?"

"I forgot to ask."

"How can you charter a vessel without knowing its name?"

I hopped on the dock to look at the transom.

"The *Mistral*," I yelled.

"The Mistress?" Ibsen yelled back.

"No darling, the *Mistral*."

"Can I take my clothes off now?"

"No, here, catch these lines . . ."

I eased the boat from its dock, still under the watchful eyes of the Scotsman who, I felt was somewhat chagrined at my crew, but when I managed to gain the main channel of the harbor without scratching her topsides he waved limply and I motored to the breakwater.

"I am going to head into the wind, Ibsen, and I want you to keep a steady course while I raise the sail."

"What do you want me to do?"

"You see that pink villa above those pines?"

"Yes?"

"Keep the bow headed that way."

I stepped to the mast and raised the mainsail, watching for tears and points of wear along the seams, but the sail was practically new, the Dacron still having sheen and stiffness, and then I raised the genoa jib and ran back to the cockpit to hold the tiller as I turned the sloop into the wind. There was a moment's immobility until the wind filled the sails. I set my sheets and felt the *Mistral* heel perhaps fifteen degrees, hull and sail becoming one moving crisply through the Mediterranean. I shut off the engine, and a quiet known only to sailors engulfed us.

I had noticed a quality in Ibsen which I dearly admired. She knew when to stay silent; It was a somewhat intellectual silence. She admitted not knowing how to sail, and yet she spared me all the embarrassing questions any skipper learns to endure when taking novices to sea. She did not comment on the compactness of the head nor wonder whether we could flip over. These were points which could be settled alone using only one's native intelligence, and Ibsen kept in character throughout our voyage, though she did display an eagerness to sail the boat herself and I tried to give her some rudimentary instructions to make it more enjoyable.

We sailed the Baie des Anges, past Cap de Nice, the swells getting a little choppier, the water a deeper and deeper blue. I could make out Cap Ferrat in the distance and did not have to rely on maps or compass to reach our destination. The wind came from starboard and I was able to set the sail so that the *Mistral* literally sailed herself.

"Let go of the tiller," I said to Ibsen, "and watch the compass."

She did as told and noticed that we were not changing direction.

"That's marvelous darling," she said. "The boat does all the work. We could make love and still reach Cap Ferrat by dinner."

"We could."

Ibsen went below and changed into her bikini. It was lemon-yellow, just two small strips of fabric, barely keeping her decent, really only heightening her nudity by its inadequacy.

She walked forward and fell asleep on the cabin top, warm and smelling of rosin from the sun.

I had begged Mary innumerable times to spend the night with me on board the *Piñata*. She was a larger boat than this little sloop, ten feet longer and a foot and a half beamier. She was comfortable and warm and steady in the water, but Mary would never join me.

"I'd feel silly sleeping on the boat when I have a perfectly good bed and perfectly good bathroom only five minutes away."

Practicality was the keyword in Mary's life, whether it would be swimming at night in Acapulco or ditching the last half of *Il Trovatore*. She was the most practical of women, her itinerary, I suspect, completely programmed at birth. I did not continuously ask for the impossible, the unusual. Perhaps in the first years of our marriage I tried, somehow, to help her lose some of her inhibitions. "Do it for me," I would plead. "Why don't you try? Why don't you at least *try?*" but even I lost my fervor. At best she would accompany a venture as a martyr, which only deprecated the experience. She was neither curious nor dissatisfied, convinced only that her methodology, be it teaching the children how to ride a bicycle or arranging books in a bookcase (The Library of Congress system) was unassailable.

It was about nine o'clock that evening and the *Mistral* was tied snugly to a buoy in the lovely harbor of St. Tropez. Ibsen had fixed a simple dinner, we had drunk much wine and brandy and were neatly tucked into our separate bunks, the light of the gimbaled kerosene lanterns casting a warm glow in the lapstraked interior of our little yacht. From my bunk I could look out the companionway, watching masts of nearby boats describing leisurely arcs in the night sky, we could hear revelers leaving and arriving on neighboring boats, but had no urge to join them either ashore or on board their boats.

Ibsen and I had discussed my marriage for the first time that evening, and I could understand, under the circumstances, her reticence in participating in the discussion, and still I persisted.

"Of course I know what is fair, Ibsen, except I find it rather silly to defend Mary when the very reason for being here negates all that."

"You're saying she's not a bitch, really, Peter. She's clean, brave and reverent. She doesn't beat children. Do you honestly think that makes her so unique?"

"I never claimed it was unique, darling."

"From what you've told me, you simply didn't fit. Why

did you persist in the marriage? Why did you have children? Why carry it on and on and on? I can't understand that?"

"There was no other place to go."

"You mean you didn't allow yourself another place to go."

"Look Ibsen, I won't deny the refugee complex. Of course security was important to me, and I was quite aware that I would have security once I married Mary . . . but there was something else."

"What?"

"My family was poor but we weren't impoverished. Does that make any sense? It should. It really should, considering what you've told me."

"Why?"

"Because you were in the same boat."

I had acquired a measure of taste in my young years. There was some elegance in our mode of living in Germany. It was only Hitler and the American Depression which made things tough for my family.

"I'm not so sure what all that has to do with your marriage?"

"I was a bright kid, Ibsen. Gentle. Not unattractive. I made friends. Close friends. Kids from Pacific Heights, Presidio Terrace. I didn't pick the neighborhood. I was first attracted to people of my own sentiments and vice versa."

"I can understand that."

"I spent many hours, lots of nights in those mansions hugging the hills near the Golden Gate watching my friends' mothers arrange the flowers in the entry hall when I knew my own was forever scrubbing the linoleum floor of an apartment kitchen. I didn't covet the money, Ibsen. I coveted the milieu. Can you believe that?"

"For a man who lives with his eyes like you do, I can, Peter. I really can."

"I wanted in. *In.* In where, who the hell knows. I was willing to trade sexuality for a butler's pantry. Love for a home down the country. Warmth for a sailboat. . . ."

"Don't talk anymore, darling."

"Why not? I'm trying to explain."

"You don't have anything to explain to me."

"I want to, Ibsen. 'Don't get heavy,' you keep saying. I *am* getting heavy. This week is drawing to a close."

"All right, Peter. You get a divorce. Gone is the house, and the second house, and probably the sailboat and the butler's pantry. Then what? Would you remain with the firm?"

"I don't know. Perhaps I could teach part time."

"Still afraid aren't you?"

"What do you mean?"

"You'd make a great teacher, Peter, I could see that this morning. But why? You shouldn't waste your time talking. You should build, build, build. Get out of that firm. They're all dependent on you. Don't you realize the reputation you have? You could get all the work you want."

I swung out of my bunk and sat next to Ibsen, pinning her arms under the blankets, kissing her face and neck.

"You think it's stupid of me to think I love you—don't answer that," I said. "You think its presumptuous of me to want you."

"Why should I think that. People have fallen in love with me before. I'm a lovely young lady. Bright, pretty, good in the sack . . ."

"Don't be facetious."

"I'm not being facetious."

"It's all very romantic darling. We're six thousand miles away from reality. It's warm, fragrant, we're on a yacht in St. Tropez—we've eaten well, drunk well, made wild love. . . . Is that how you want to continue to live Ibsen? One affair after another?"

"No Peter. I'm looking for something, too. We're all looking for something."

"I know," I said. "Come on, let's take a swim."

Ibsen jumped out of bed; she was naked and up the companionway before I knew it.

"Last one in is a dirty old maid."

I heard her dive into the water and followed her in. The water was still warm and black as ink. Our bodies floating on its surface looking ghostly and fragile, the *Mistral* quite beautiful riding the gentle swells with great compassion.

"Do you always run around naked?" I asked Ibsen as we were toweling ourselves dry on the stern of the boat.

"Whenever I get a chance."

"Do you run around naked in Sausalito?"

"I do at home. The milkman and I are old friends."

"I'll bet."

"Dry my back."

"Oooh, that feels good. You know what you can do now?"

"What?"

"You can put some lotion on it."

We went below and Ibsen handed me a bottle of white lotion and stretched onto her stomach. I opened the bottle and painted a straight line of the creamy, fragrant liquid from the nape of her neck to her fanny.

"Oooh, that is cold."

I spread the lotion evenly over her back, rubbing it firmly into the skin until her back took on a lovely sheen in the kerosene light.

"Peter."

"Shut up." I poured lotion down the length of the backs of her legs, working it carefully into her feet, her calves, her thighs, then I flipped her over and poured lotion on her nipples like decorating a birthday cake with icing. I spread the lotion in ever-widening circles over her breasts.

"Peter Trowbridge, you, you are driving me insane."

"Wait til I get to the fun parts."

"Where do you think you are now?"

"Be quiet."

I poured lotion on her neck and into her ear and drenched her clitoris until all of her felt like a syrupy nymph, thus totally undone, only the confinement of the bunk allowed us to make love at all, we were both so lotioned, as slippery as eels.

"You owe me a bottle of lotion," Ibsen said before falling asleep.

"My hands aren't at all chapped anymore."

The sun poured on my face and I gently disengaged myself from Ibsen, feeling neither middle-aged nor hung over, but rather proud that I could still sleep as I had, practically off the bunk, one leg over the flag locker, without experiencing a great deal of stiffness. I found my bathing trunks, put them on and went topside. A number of other yachts had come in to the harbor during the night, the *Mistral* looked very chipper in a gay, early morning light. I found a bar of soap and lowered myself down the boarding ladder and bathed in the salt water with a certain amount of difficulty, then washed down the teak decks with great energetic splashes of seawater from a canvas bucket.

"Hey, Captain Bligh," Ibsen stuck her head out of the skylight, dripping wet, "what are you trying to do? Drown me?"

"Up, up and away."

Ibsen disappeared into the cabin, then came out wrapped in an orange beach towel, still rubbing her hair.

"I want to speak to the Captain."

"Jus' doin' mah job, Missa."

"I had the most wonderful dream. I had just received the Oscar for the sets in *Weekend*. There I was, Poitier handed it to me, and then I dove right off this boat into a whole ocean filled with hand lotion."

"What libidinous rot."

"It was great until some jerk poured salt water onto my face."

"Come on," I said, "make some breakfast. We've got a long sail ahead of us."

I motored to the first open quay in St. Tropez, bought ice, a bouquet of hothouse tulips, six freshly baked baguettes of bread, salami, a good small etching, and returned to the *Mistral*, fragrant with scents of bacon and fresh coffee emanating from the cabin.

136

"You know," I said, "I still have most of the money I brought over here. Why don't we just keep sailing. The coast of Africa, the Azores, down the Bahamas, the Lesser Antilles."

"How long would it take?"

"Six months, a year . . ."

"Well, how much did it cost to charter this boat?"

"A hundred dollars a day."

"Well, a hundred dollars a day, three hundred and sixty-five bottles of hand lotion."

"Come on—let's have some chow."

We ate, I checked the halyards to make certain they were running free, headed the *Mistral* to the mouth of the harbor, raised the sail and took the first tack toward Nice. I guessed the winds at twenty knots. We both put on sweaters, little whitecaps appeared and an occasional swell spilled overboard, the water running alongside the cabin deck and out the scuppers.

"It seems like we're going much faster today Peter."

"It's an illusion. When you're heading into the wind the boat works much harder."

"Let me take the tiller."

"There, and watch that ribbon on the stay. Keep it at a forty-five degree angle to the bow. If you see it flutter you're going too close. Then the sails will luff and the boat will stop."

"Aye, aye. Boy, that's hard to hold."

"There's lots of pressure on that rudder."

I walked forward and sat on the pulpit and watched the *Mistral* slice cleanly through the dark-blue water, the foamy quarterwave leaving the boat in ever-widening symmetry, and then turned around and admired the apposition of the tightly drawn genoa jib against the main, the lovely pattern of sail against sail and sail against sky, the stays and halyards almost contrapuntal in their configuration, and my eyes traveled further to Ibsen in the cockpit, her legs braced against the starboard seat, her arms straight and straining against the tiller, her hair free and lovely rivaling the movement of the tricolor flying from our stern. She belonged. She looked as clean and fit as the ship she was sailing.

"I can see what you mean about boats, Peter. I've been looking around. They are truly beautiful."

"Of course they are. Buildings could be beautiful too. The biggest problem is that architecture is not really a profession."

"Here, here. I spent a lot of years in school, Peter."

"Of course you did, and so did I and we got degrees and membership in the AIA and God knows, but the average practitioner has very little control over his destiny.

"We are ruled by greed. Not *our* greed entirely, but the greed of the developers. A man buys a lot. The price of the lot determines the height of the building. No architectural control. He wants the greatest amount of square footage his money will buy. Ergo, a rectangle or a cube. What is the function of the architect? To pick the moldings? The shape of the windows? The color of the lobby? Any fag decorator can do this."

"You've got to be realistic, darling."

"I *am* realistic. There are enough men who can do a decent building, but they never get the chance. The bank, the savings and loan institution, the building commissioners, the investors. We're all whores. You don't tell a surgeon how to remove a lung or an attorney how to defend a murderer."

"You can't blame the little architect trying to make a living?"

"I *do* blame him. The little ones and the big ones. Where the hell is the AIA? If a man wants an architect to build his building then the architect should be in charge. If the client doesn't like it, then refuse the commission."

"You can do that Peter, because people want a Trowbridge building. Perhaps it's a matter of natural selection. Only the good architects can exercise some independence."

"Then the poor ones should be thrown out of the profession. Even a badly built structure can offend the eye for sixty–seventy years—I am sick, Ibsen, sick of it. All around us are our monuments of poor design."

"Is it true that you built the city hall in Evenforest in the shape of a toilet?"

"Only if you view it from the air. The whole administration was controlled by the Mafia."

"Didn't they try to sue?"

"They did sue. We won. We merely argued that there was nothing ugly about toilets."

"You really puzzle me."

"Why?"

"You're such a contradictory man. You're absolutely ruthless about your work. When I first met you at Wolf Ranch I was a little afraid of you."

"Me?"

"Yes. I'd never met you. I'd only read about you. Read your articles in the Journal. You're a very angry young man in the literature."

"And what was it like when you met me? Was I a boob?"

"Not a boob. A child, but maybe you've got just the right kind of combination. Maybe you need that domestic frustration to function as well as you do in architecture."

"To hell with that Ibsen."

"Sure, you say that today."

"Why can't a man function when he's happy?"

"Maybe he is dividing his passions."

"If you don't pull up those bikini pants, I'll divide some passion right now."

I looked at my watch, and my compass, studied the chart which I had found below, then the coastline.

"I think we can make our last tack and come right to the lighthouse." I turned the tiller toward the boom and held it until the bow of the *Mistral* headed into the wind. I let go the genoa sheet and watched the large sail work itself around the forward stay like children hiding behind full-length drapes. The boat swung easily. I tightened the sheets, we were very close-hauled, the boat heeled practically to the waterline.

It was almost dusk when we reached the lighthouse. The ocean was turning orange and red, the wind dying, the air still warm and more fragrant the closer we came to shore. I dropped the sails, stowed the genoa and slowly approached our mooring. I expected to see the Scotsman nervously pacing, but he was not there. A young man, clean-cut, perhaps thirty years old, wearing denims and sneakers, a blue-and-white striped cardigan sat on a shore box on our dock.

"We've got a welcoming committee," I said.

"Oh God," Ibsen said. "It's John Perry."

"Take the stern line," I said, handing it to Ibsen. She took it out of my hand and said, "You've got to believe me darling, I didn't know he was coming."

I came in slowly, reversing the engine at the last minute and brought the *Mistral* to rest without touching the dock.

"That's very expert seamanship," the man on the dock yelled as I walked forward to tie the towlines.

"I am John Perry."

"Peter Trowbridge."

"The architect?"

I bent down to tie the lines and did not answer him, returning to the cockpit.

Perry followed me, yelling cheerfully, "Hello I.I."

"Hello John."

"I'd like permission to board."

"I bet you would."

Ibsen looked at me. She was half amused by my remark, half perplexed as what to do.

"I bring greetings from Chester, Maybelline, the Thurmonds; Eloise is pregnant again, Gilbert won the Parkhurst Regatta, Dean Rusk asks to be remembered, let's see," Perry said. "I suppose that brings you up to date in Georgetown."

I coiled the main sheet and hung it at the end of the boom and snapped the sail covers in place. I shut off gas and water in the engines, doused our running lights, took down the tricolor and hoped somehow for endless numbers of chores to keep from thinking.

"We sailed to St. Tropez," Ibsen said. "Spent the night. It was lovely."

"Did you eat at Auberge?"

"We didn't leave the boat."

"I hear it's gone downhill."

"You got my wires?"

"I did. Shall we all have a drink?"

Ibsen went below, then returned. "We only have wine."

"Anything," Perry said trying desparately to engage me in the conversation, but I still managed to find a few things to keep me busy so not to have to face him in the cockpit.

Ibsen came up from the cabin with a bottle of red wine, three glasses, and we each raised them in a silent toast.

"I am a great admirer of yours Mr. Trowbridge. The Embassy in Pakistan is an absolute jewel. A handsome embassy is the best introduction to meaningful diplomacy."

"What do you do, Mr. Perry?"

"I'm a foreign service officer."

"I see."

There was silence and Perry, stirring a little uncomfortably, started. "Since diplomacy is really my business, I suppose I should explain this intrusion."

"Don't," Ibsen commanded quite sternly.

"The two of you looked so convivial bringing your boat in."

"We were, John. We are."

"Could we have dinner together? Would you all be my

guests? I'm at the Hotel de Paris. How about tonight? You're staying at Pension Aida?"

"I don't think either of us feel like getting dressed tonight, John. How long are you staying?"

"I don't know."

"Why don't you give us a ring tomorrow. Not too early. Maybe we can have lunch at the beach or something."

"I've been flying for fourteen hours, I suppose a night's sleep won't hurt me either." He finished his wine in one gulp and stood up, extended his hand toward me.

"I do hope I get a chance to talk to you Mr. Trowbridge." He leaned down and kissed Ibsen on the cheek. "You look absolutely marvelous."

"Ciào," Ibsen waved as he disappeared down the dock.

"Ciào," he said trying to look carefree, youthful, debonair. I almost felt sorry for him.

Ibsen went below gathering the few stores remaining from our voyage, rolled up the bedding and handed me our small canvas satchel. We stepped ashore, pausing for a minute to admire the *Mistral* once more, to bid farewell, as it were.

"I loved the sail Peter, thank you."

"She's very yawr. Remember that line from *Philadelphia Story?*"

We kissed and Ibsen put her arm in mine and we walked purposefully to Pension Aida.

We showered, I made a couple of vermouth cassis and we stood on our balcony, toasting the sea which had borne us so well for two days.

143

"I appreciate your getting us out of dinner with your friend, Ibsen, but I am sort of hungry."

"Let's go to Le Comargue. I know the owners."

"Perhaps we'll run into your friend. Maybe he won't want to dine alone at the hotel."

"Maybe we will, I can handle that."

I looked confused, I knew, and Ibsen recognized it.

"I'll tell you all about it, darling. Maybe over dinner. Don't look so pouty."

"It is so stupid of me Ibsen, I know that. What did I expect? To find you all wrapped in cellophane at Wolf Ranch, like a fresh pack of cigarettes—no past, no present, ready, waiting. What am I trying to do? Erase twenty-six years?"

"You're being very sweet."

"I'm not. I'm jealous as hell. Who is this guy? Who is Albert Kahn? What do they want from you? What does everybody want?"

"What would you like me to wear?"

"Something sexy, low-cut, low-necked, short-skirted."

"Every time I ask you this question, you give me the same answer."

Le Comargue on Rue du Banque consisted of only two chambers: a bar which held a great circular couch, covered with shorn horsehide, a round coffee table in its center with a lovely crystal punch bowl filled with a spicy concoction, cloves, cinnamon, rum, brandy; and the dining room which by its simplicity became quite elegant. The walls were of natural brick, whitewashed—there were perhaps twenty circular tables with red-and-white checkered cloths, a large open fireplace and butcher-block table in one corner; all of it lit by tiny, brass kerosene lanterns; an elderly Spaniard sat on a low stool playing songs of Andalusia on the guitar. Simply framed Picasso bullfight drawings graced one wall; it was a lovely, intimate room, and the owners, a couple Ibsen's age, were equally attractive and accommodating.

We drank more punch than we should have and staggered to our table where a great bowl of fresh, raw vegetables awaited us. We ordered steak tartare, red wine, both of us glowing from the alcohol and the Mediterranean sun. Ibsen had obliged me by wearing a perforated minidress.

"If you bought that dress by weight, you were cheated. Did they make you pay for the holes?"

"Aren't they clever. Look, if I move quickly I can come right through it."

I held her hands as if to restrain that maneuver and Ibsen only laughed.

"You're so possessive Peter."

"I know, I know."

"I'm really rather proud of those bosoms."

"So am I. Do you have to share them?"

"Just a few close friends."

"Speaking of a few close friends."

"I know, I know, darling. John Perry."

"What about him?"

"Wouldn't you rather let me tell you about him when we're in bed, then I can sort of squirm around all over the place, put my feet up on the wall?"

"You know how much talking we'll get done under those circumstances."

"I keep forgetting, you're so frustrated."

"I'm frustrated?"

"Well, I admit to nymphomania, but what is your excuse?"

"All those barren years."

" 'All those barren years,' " Ibsen imitated my voice. "All those barren years, my foot. You must have learned how to make love somewhere."

"You're still dodging the question."

"I am, aren't I."

"Aren't you?"

"Is this *vin ordinaire?*"

"All you can drink darling, prix fixe."

"Twenty dollars prix fixe. The Riviera is such a bargain."

"I met John Perry at the Annual Advertising Awards Dinner at the Plaza Hotel in New York. One of my theater posters won an honorable mention."

"Good."

"Yes, good. He presented himself after dinner, quite elegantly, complimented my work and handed me his card. It said the Plow and Angel Press. A pretty card really. They were doing a book on theater art."

"I thought he was in the Foreign Service."

"He is. He and a group of friends owned a small press to work off their creative urges. More wine?"

"More wine."

"Isn't this tartare delicious?"

"Delicious."

"Anyhow, I tucked his little card into my cleavage and promptly forgot Mr. Perry, the Plow and Angel Press, the fact that I had lost an earring that evening, and that was that until he presented himself at my doorstep the following day. I was living in the village at the time—all homemade cornbread, antiwar posters, black stockings, you know."

"I know," I said and laughed, "he came to see your etchings."

"Precisely. Well, to make a long story tolerable, I should say that John Perry was, or, for that matter, is a very brilliant young man."

"Go on."

"No, really Peter. He's Boston Brahmin, superbly educated, Exeter, Harvard, Oxford, the Sorbonne, just a beautiful schooling; and he is artistic, and he does have a sense of humor . . . taste, what can I say?"

"You say anymore, I'll hit you with this empty bottle."

"Well, we dated, and he'd run up from Washington on the shuttle in the evenings and I would go visit him there on weekends and there was a lot of traveling and eating on the run and getting up at five in the morning, and parties and balls, you know, my world, art, architecture, show biz; his world, politics, power, intrigue. Lots of good talk, lots of bright people . . . and one morning, a cold, dreary Monday morning in Washington, I said, screw it."

"You, my baby Ibsen said *that?*"

"I, your baby Ibsen said that, more wine. I, I Ibsen Iazzo, I said, you're getting drunk. Peter, I, Ibsen Iazzo said screw it. I am not going on that goddamn shuttle this morning. I am turning into a shuttle whore. I am either going to stay here, or I am going to shuttle home and stay home!" Ibsen lowered her head to punctuate her statement. "And so—so

John Perry, the gallant John Perry said, 'Stay here.' And I said, 'I will,' and turned over and went to sleep. And I stayed a year. That was last year."

"I see."

"What do you mean 'I see'?"

"I mean I see. You stayed a year."

"No, no, Peter darling." Ibsen stood up. "Do you mind if I sit next to you? We're not having a seminar." She moved from her side of the table and sat on the bench next to me. "What the hell is it with you?"

"What do you mean?"

" 'I see,' you said. You see nothing. What would you like to do? Just torture yourself that Perry and I had this great libidinous year? That I just stayed in bed the whole time waiting for him to come home with a hard-on?"

"I am forty-two, Ibsen. How old is Perry?"

"Twenty-eight."

"All right. He's twenty-eight. What would you like me to do? Ask a lot of foolish questions?"

"Why not? Does forty-two put you out of the running?"

"You tell me . . ."

"Nothing heavy."

"Nothing heavy. Your favorite expression."

"I'm sorry. I'm only trying to tell you not to sit there like some goddamned injustice collector. There is a denouement."

"A denouement. Very good. You've not only lived a full life, but you have a rich and varied vocabulary."

"Stop being coy, Peter Trowbridge. There. I knew I would do it."

"Do what?"

"Look!"

"Oh for Christsakes." Ibsen had now managed to coincide both nipples with her perforated dress. I pulled the dress up at the neckline.

"Do we really have to go on about John Perry?"

"No."

"Yes, we do. You see," Ibsen leveled a none too steady finger at me, "the first question that boy asked me after I awoke that first morning should really have been a clue. He asked, 'What about your career Ibsen,' and I said, 'Which one,' but I don't think he caught on. 'Your set designing. You've got a million projects lined up.' 'So,' I said, 'I will unline a million projects.' 'But what about the momentum?' he asked, and I said, 'What's wrong with my momentum? Didn't you come last night?' "

The waiter returned with the check, and I paid and felt a little foolish in the now-empty dining room.

"I think we have closed up Le Comargue."

"What would you like to do Peter?"

"Take a walk."

"Would you like to see two colored girls make love to a goat?"

"No."

"Would you like to drop a quick thousand dollars at the Casino? You only need a Shell Oil credit card to get in?"

"No."

We stood and fussed over the meal with the owner, we promised to return, we wrapped Ibsen's luminescent bosoms into an orange shawl, refused brandy, Pernod, crème de menthe and walked aimlessly toward the harbor.

"Did you lock the *Mistral*, darling?"

"Not with a key."

"Do you think we could sneak on board?"

"We could try."

"Let's."

We found the boat and the dock quite solitary. I climbed on board, slid back the hatch cover and we let ourselves into the cabin undetected. There was enough moonlight to give us a sense of direction. I found a blanket in the forward locker, a sailbag for a pillow, and we lay down on the starboard bunk.

"Is your boat as pretty as this one Peter?"

"Prettier."

"Is it yours or is it Mary's?"

"It belongs to the Chemical Bank of New York."

"That's right, I forgot. Who do you belong to?"

Ibsen passed out in my arms and I managed only to pull off her shoes, tucking the coarse, woolen blanket about both of us. I was heavy and leaden with red wine myself, juxtaposing the presence of Perry in Nice, the waning days of our week, my distance from home and reality with slow, ponderous reasoning. I reached under the blanket for Ibsen's breasts, still warm but somewhat flaccid, and tried to sort out my feelings, but found it unlike a set of specs to be neatly drawn on the bottom of a blueprint, more like an endless series of circles, there was that firmament of love for Ibsen. I could feel her, I could smell her, I could hear her, her long, soft hair in my face and on my neck and chest, and from that firmament radiated hope and youth and warmth and joy and laughter, much laughter, and there were wedges of doubt, of fear and guilt and there were shafts of jealousy and violence, of dark corners and uncertainty. Who was Ibsen. What was Ibsen. Was this my price for being good? Good for what? For whom? No—no. Good architect. Good, honest architect. Good, honest design. Good, honest buildings. Good, honest cheating husband, father. Yes, Mr. Perry I am a much-married man. Yes, Mr. Perry, I am a little old for this sort of thing. Yes, Mr. Perry. Who's Mr. Perry? Mary, who is Mr. Perry? Ibsen, who is Mary? I will tell the Scotsman I lost my watch in his boat. Right Mr. Perry? Lost it all night. Tick tock. Up the wall, down the ceiling, down the wall . . . tick tock. Tick tock.

We woke at dawn, climbed out of the cabin like thieves, found a cab that took us to Pension Aida. It was already warm on our terrace. Ibsen puttered about making coffee, we were both a little weary and hung over, decided to forego the sun and finally collapsed in bed. The phone woke us at eleven o'clock. It was John Perry and Ibsen told him of our night and begged off seeing him.

"Thank you, darling," I said.

"You're welcome."

"What about the denouement?"

"What denouement?"

"Between Ibsen Iazzo and Mr. John Perry."

"This early in the morning? Stop that."

"You're trying to paper the issue."

"I'm not."

"There's still a spark."

151

"There's not."

"Then why the mystery?"

"My week is coming to a close, too, Peter."

I turned over in bed.

"Ibsen?"

"Yes?"

"What the hell is a foreign service officer?"

"John is an Assistant Secretary of State."

"Oh. Well, I'm glad he's in management."

Ibsen drew next to me. "I love you, you dumb bastard."

Yeah. Protocol.

13

MORNING brought brioche and café au lait, a handwritten, hand-delivered invitation to a party aboard the Kahn yacht that evening. Ibsen refused to wake up, I dressed and walked slowly out of the room. I bought pastry, cheese, sausage, a bunch of hyacinths, and a copy of *Paris-Match* and sat quietly in the gardens of the Musée Massena and watched two boys, I guessed their age to be seven, playing with miniature automobiles. They were neatly dressed and managed to propel their cars on the little dirt path without soiling their clothes. I thought of my own children and the acres and acres of land they consumed to amuse themselves and wondered whether all the vastness, the waste, the primitiveness of America was detrimental, whether all that abundance only created vacuity, whether millions of acres of wheat swaying in a summer breeze created smugness, an endless array of leisure toys, boredom. Perhaps there was more here—France, Italy, Portugal, Spain, England, Ireland, Scotland, Wales, Denmark, Sweden . . . bloodstained blood-drenched ground, crossed and recrossed by armies, ruled and overthrown by Church and State, land with heritage, land with culture, soil tilled and retilled, families with lineage and tradition.

The two young boys rose and frugally brushed their clothes with their hands. They returned their small toy cars into the pockets of their blazers, held hands and started to leave. They paused for a minute to look at me, foreign and intrusive, and then they left the park, half walking, half running, across the Promenade des Anglais and then they disappeared and I wanted to cry out, no, I am not foreign, I am not strange. I understand.

What was it Ibsen had said? John Perry is twenty-eight, and you are forty-two. Does that put you out of the running? It was a fair question, and yet I did not know how to answer it.

I WAS BORN in a rigid, aseptic middle-class home with an- cestral chinaware displayed in massive fruitwood cabinets; velvet drapes and ponderous oil paintings of half-balding red-headed ancestors in stiff collared tunics. It was all pon- derous, massive and carved and seemed in retrospect to represent nothing more than an elaborate labyrinth which necessitated endless dusting, scrubbing, polishing, waxing. But these were the memories of childhood: the scrub brush, the washboard, large bars of gleaming handmade soap, ladders and chamois, the smell of ammonia and clothes being boiled in tin vats in the basement and hung to dry on clotheslines in the attic like sails in a sailmakers loft. There was cleanliness and antiquity and much fresh air, long boring walks in the Schwartzwald, hikes to the municipal park, endless marches to the dentist; there was good healthy food, greens and fruits and fresh sausage and warm rolls for breakfast, there was Christmas and Christmas trees with burning wax candles and Lebkuchen and Pfeffernüsse, but there was no talk of sex. There was no real affection between my parents. There was no interplay, no random domestic nudity. Bathrooms were like operating rooms, sterile, private and locked, and bedrooms were chambers which held massive carved wooden beds covered with eiderdowns and down coverlets, furniture which resembled massive caskets lacking only floral sprays and organ music. It was all cold and aseptic, only a few shafts of stimulation, like sunlight in a well would pierce my childhood: a communal bath with a female cousin, a drunken chambermaid doing an amateur can-can while my parents were at a concert. I can only recall my last evening in Germany, our home torn up, the possessions of a lifetime plundered by relatives and friends, the paintings gone, the books bequeathed, the china and silverware doled out to anxious eager neighbors; a curious sensual night.

It had taken a week after the receipt of the visas in Nuremberg to secure passage on a ship to America. One week in which to dispose of a lifetime of associations, a lifetime of possessions. One week to bid farewell to friends and relatives, a farewell as final as seeing them at the edge of a freshly dug grave.

I had watched the procession through our home. Friends and relatives, business associates eating pastries, drinking coffee, wine; much good vintage Rhine wine hoarded for future celebrations, weddings, births and graduation, now poured contemptuously to rob some goddamn Nazi of the pleasure in the future.

They came like locusts and they shed tears and carried away treasure. One a chest, another a chair, a dining room table, a divan, an oil painting, a bronze statuary; pots, pans dishes, linen, silver, pewter, dress shirts, books and bedsteads, lamps, walking sticks, gramophones, bound volumes of well-kept magazines. And I dispensed toys. Trains, trucks and motor scooters, teddy bears, collections of rocks, minerals, and random stamps. A music box. A swing. A scale replica of the Graf Zeppelin and a cuckoo clock whose pine cones and trusty bird had measured my young years like a pacemaker in a troubled heart.

It was the last night and our house was barren save for the suitcases poised for departure in the front hall. Only a bed remained in my parents' bedroom and a few belongings not yet plundered or unwanted by the intruders. There was to be a celebration in my parents' home. The last of the wine was to be drunk from the cellar, the last of the crystal to be smashed against the hearth, and I was ferried to neighbors, perhaps to shield me against further trauma, perhaps to save me from embarrassment in seeing my parents drunk.

The Warburgs had been good friends of the family, their daughter Erika two years my senior a constant companion since infancy. She was a pretty girl, or how does one remember. Her hair brunette and cut very short in a bob, her skin so fair, her figure short, she was and had been as close as if she were my sister, sharing all the games, the projects, the activities of our own coterie. We had allied and we had fought and we had confided and conspired but it was not until this night, this last night in Germany, this last night in my own hometown that we shared a bedroom; innocently lying in twin beds while her parents attended the rites in my own, so barren home.

We had talked, as we had done so many times before into the quiet hours of early morning, but this night Erika asked more and spoke less. She tried I know to tell me in her own adolescent way that she loved me, that she did not want me to go away, that she would miss me, and I knew that even at twelve I felt warm and strange and mysterious, and when she impetuously left her bed and jumped into mine, when she kissed me as I had never been kissed before, when I held her young, firm breasts under her chaste flannel nightgown, I knew not what ecstacy I was experiencing because I could not quite believe it, but there, that night, the rite of passage was beginning, this last evening in my homeland, a frail beautiful child gave me life and sustenance beyond any I had ever known in that barren country. I had felt her tears and her cheeks and her lips and her arms, and when dawn spread light into our room and I pulled on the clothes for our departure, when I stood with my parents in front of our house waiting for the driver to take us to the train depot, when all the relatives and friends embraced me one more time, pressed one more candy bar into my hand, a little marzipan for the trip, a silver key chain, I left only one little girl, and one embrace, and one set of tears. In some areas, for me, it was a beginning, and not the end.

Still passage to America did not signal the beginning of manhood for me; the new language, the new customs, endless new faces helped only to instill shyness in me, perhaps suspicion, distrust; and where a John Perry could flow easily from football field to soda fountain, from the junior prom to the back seat of his father's Buick, for me those years of high school were totally graceless, my emphasis more on survival than conquest. As it had from time immemorial, the immigrant's hope lay in an education and my parents followed the classic rule.

They saw no value in frivolity, they cared little about my adolescence, they were bewildered themselves; it was as if we were on a night patrol through the jungle. You looked neither right nor left. You did not stop to rest. You did not speak to the man ahead of you or the man behind. You marched. Propelled by fear, you marched.

It was not a totally monastic existence. I don't mean to imply that. I dated girls rarely, clumsily. I had little finesse and even less money. At 14 I snuck into the Geary Theater with friends, rushing the Chinaman for the front seat at the end of the movie to watch the burlesque show. I stared at the veiled breasts and fannies, at the shaved pubic areas of sad older girls in the harsh light of a pink spot; but when I met Mary, when our courtship more by years than passion formalized in marriage, I was no veteran of countless affairs, no wiser from endless romances. Watching John Perry step gracefully aboard the *Mistral* yesterday, noting his composure, no matter how well figured, I felt not older than he, but younger. More inept, less surefooted. I felt more kinship with the two youngsters who had just departed, running toward Nice.

❧

I CAME BACK to the pension and found Ibsen hanging our underwear on a clothesline which extended from our patio to the house across the street.

"Here they are, Peter Trowbridge, your underpants and my bikini panties side by side across Rue des Bac."

"How brash can you get?"

"There is our infidelity waving in the breeze, our sins displayed as gaily as a children's carnival."

I looked at the laundry waving briskly and the clouds building over the Mediterranean.

"Those are rain clouds," I said.

"Really?"

"Your laundry will never dry."

"Then we shan't be able to go home . . ."

"That's right. Dear Mary, since my shorts have not dried completely, this letter is to inform you . . ."

"Blah, blah, blah, blah."

"The airlines phoned to confirm our reservation while you were out."

"We leave in forty-eight hours."

"I know, Peter. Shut up, will you."

"What did I say?"

"Nothing." Ibsen kissed me. "Let's go to the beach."

"What about John Perry?"

"Forget him. He'll probably be at Kahn's tonight."

"Are we going?"

"We should. I still have to get that yacht for a week."

I did not pursue it. We took our towels and walked to the beach. It was relatively empty. A few tourists, a few children.

"Does your boy want to be an architect, Peter?"

"No."

"What does he want to be?"

"He doesn't know."

"Is he talented?"

"I couldn't tell you."

"You never talk about your children."

"I know."

"Are you ashamed of yourself, being here with me? Is that the reason?"

"No, darling."

"What is it then?"

"I don't know them. Not really. It's my fault as much as their's. Mary is a very domineering woman. A good mother, I suppose. Mary has all the credentials. A good mother, a good wife, a good cook, a good manager. Plays a decent game of golf, an excellent game of bridge . . ."

"To hell with Mary. Tell me about the children."

"They are pleasant looking. They are well behaved. They think of me as rather a weak man, I suppose, who rarely interferes. . . . They come home from school occasionally, talk to me uncomfortably for about a half an hour and continue their own activities."

"They weren't always away at school. They must have been little once?"

"They were, and I loved them, Ibsen. What can I tell you? I've always loved them. Why all these questions about my children?"

"It's important to me how a man feels about children. How would you feel about another child?"

"With you?'

"With me."

"Is it imminent?"

"It could be. We haven't exactly been practicing the rhythm method."

"I think I'd be ready for another child. Have you ever been pregnant, Ibsen?"

"Once. Yes. John Perry. . . ." Ibsen looked at me. "I can talk about it, Peter. Now I can!"

"You don't have to."

"No, but I owe you that."

"You owe me nothing, darling. This has been the greatest week in my life."

"I stayed in Washington and I kept John Perry's house. I cooked and washed and ironed, I made love to him and he to me. We saw plays and listened to concerts, we made the rounds of embassies and legations. The White House, Blair

House, and the eight floors of Foggy Bottom. I was charming, elegant, demure, coquettish. I was loving, and discreet; it was good. For the most part it was good.

"We talked of marriage and agreed to play it by ear. I had moved in with him in December. In June I was pregnant. Not on purpose, not by any connivance. It happened. It does." Ibsen was sifting sand from one hand to another, looking far out to sea. "I was happy. Very happy. I wanted the baby. I loved John. At best it finalized our plans."

"He didn't want the child?"

"He didn't want the child. He didn't want me! He spoke of his career. Only his career. The relative value of his unattached status in the Washington Scene. 'It carries weight, Ibsen,' he said. 'Can't you see that? I am still eligible. It gives me a certain leverage.'

"It was all handled very elegantly, Peter. A friend of the family in Boston, a professor of OB and GYN at Harvard, no less. Flowers, a private room, books, candy. I walked out as soon as my head cleared from the anesthesia."

"You haven't seen him since?"

"Twice. He's been phoning, wiring, writing. I made a lot of friends in Washington. I hear I'm missed."

"Then how did he know you would be here?"

"He phoned the studio I suppose. He knows his way around."

"But he didn't expect *me* here."

"Obviously not."

"Look, Ibsen, I am not terribly good at these soigné affairs, these confrontation scenes."

"Darling, this is not a confrontation scene. John Perry is

162

dead. I am going to the Kahn yacht to get permission to use it for *Weekend*. Screw everybody else."

"There are men who gain commissions at cocktail parties," I said. "I call them cocktail architects. I've seen them operate. It doesn't matter what building I have completed, no matter how successful the job has been, I bungle it at the festivities."

"You don't need that sort of thing, Peter. Your work speaks for you."

"That's a very kind thing to say, Ibsen, but there is something deeper about my behavior. Whether I am intimidated by money or position, I don't know.

"We had a maid working for us in Germany. It wasn't a status symbol. All middle-class families had maids. They were poor farm girls who came into the city, slaved ten hours a day, were paid practically nothing. Once on her day off she took me to visit her sister since she had children my age. They lived in the most meager of circumstances, I can't recall the details, only the pastries."

"The pastries?"

"I had played with the sister's children and at four o'clock we were called in for coffee. This was the custom. Strong black coffee filled with thick gobs of whipped cream. There were two chocolate pastries in a box which was ceremoniously opened and the pastry put on my plate. I wanted to share the pastry with the other children but was told no, and I remember the mocking tone, *das ist für den Sohn der Herrschaft*, for the son of the boss, and I almost choked consuming the cakes under the hateful eyes of the other children, the maid, her sister. I have been in homes like the presidents of steel companies, oil companies, presidents of universities, kings, dukes, ambassadors . . . I have this fear, this dread that I am exhibiting the same kind of hunger as those little boys watching me eat the pastry."

"But you married a rich girl. Why? It seems like an obvious need to torture yourself."

"I've explained some of it, Ibsen. I liked the milieu, I've told you that. I was green. I was led. I knew the girl would please my parents. Unsure of myself. Perhaps I was hoping that it would all work out."

"Did you ever get any help? Professional help, I mean."

"You mean an analyst?"

"Yes."

"A little. Surprises you, doesn't it?"

"No."

"I mean the rigid German."

"You're not a rigid German, darling. *I* saw one right after the abortion . . . what did he say when you saw yours, Peter?"

"Get a divorce. What about you, Ibsen? Could you be totally open? Could you undress your soul the way you leave off your clothes?"

"Not quite, Peter. There was no father in my household. My mother was a bright, jolly articulate woman, to be sure, and I adored her, but she was still quite midwestern in her morality. She knew Freud existed and Jung and she heard about Krafft-Ebing at faculty lunches, but for the most part she was straight, rigid. 'Don't wear that slip, Ibsen, I can see your legs right through the dress.' 'You're reading

164

de Maupassant, Ibsen? Just remember that most of those Frenchmen had syphilis and all those terrible diseases. Why don't you get on your bicycle and put a little fresh air into your chest.' "

"But you overcame all that. You became a free spirit. Emancipated, liberated, independent, carefree."

"Don't be so sure, Peter."

Ibsen turned her head to kiss me, then stretched out on her towel and gave herself to the sun. She was asleep in a matter of minutes.

I HAD NEVER been able to understand Mary completely. As I had matured in my profession the honors certainly materalized, but I was neither covetous of prizes nor could I quite understand my growing eminence in the profession of architecture.

Perhaps the best that I could say was that I was blessed with an innate talent. I apparently had an eye. I knew how long a building should be, and how high, I had a feel for texture, for relief, for starkness and playfulness. I was well-grounded classically and could draw on the best works of my predecessors for guidance and reference, and yet I knew I had a boldness of my own, an inner vision.

I did not stand in awe of these gifts, I accepted them and used them. I did not ask my associates to recognize me, which they did, I did not openly beg for critique which I received internationally, I did not set out to be a wunderkind in architecture, which I was, nor a cause célèbre every time I completed a project, which I also became. I did not, truly, ask for these things.

And yet, accepting these facts of life, it was rather curious that Mary reacted so nonchalantly to all that happened to me. She accompanied me to openings and to showings of my works, she dutifully read the endless stories about my accomplishments, she heard the praises of my clients and colleagues, and yet she reacted ever more coolly, as if to say, well, he is an architect. I suppose the thing to do is to be a good one.

Accomplishment after accomplishment was somehow compared to yet another merger which her father had accomplished, another merchant triumph which he had pulled off.

Danner, no doubt, was an astute businessman. He had taken his father's million-dollar legacy and built it into an empire, but I was neither in competition with Danner nor felt that Mary's position as his daughter gave her the right to be so unsupportive of my own accomplishment.

THE STORM was building off the coast and the clouds finally covered the sun. Ibsen's lovely browned body turned to goose bumps. I tousled her hair to waken her, she huddled next to me.

"Boy, what happened to the sunny Riviera?"

"God has spoken. Enough, you sinners."

"To hell with that, Peter. Let's find some wood and build

a fire in our bedroom. We've got that great Meissen stove."

We gathered driftwood on the beach, picked up our towels and climbed the time-worn stone steps to Pension Aida. I could not tear myself from the veranda. The ocean was changing colors continuously. Blues and grays and blacks, white foam, splotches of sunlight still in the distance, and finally came lightning and thunder and the great bulbous menacing rain clouds sending sheets of water, drenching the veranda and the streets and gutters, the ancient rain spouts, the aging acacias, the bougainvillea, the nasturtiums, the begonias, the children running home from school, all things living or dead, washed and abused by the torrents of rain.

Ibsen had set a fire in the old Meissen stove, lighting the shavings as I came in from the veranda. I found a bottle of red wine, some cheese and bread from my morning walk and we settled on the floor, *le Picnique* as Ibsen said, watching the inclement weather outside.

"I'm happy about this storm," Ibsen said. "The weather was really getting to be blah."

"Yes, just that rotten sunshine all the time."

"Don't you like rain, darling?"

"Today I do."

Ibsen had taken off her bathing suit and slipped into one of my shirts. It barely covered her as she sat on the floor with her usual abandon. She was brushing her hair and I watched as she followed each strand from the crown of her head to its end below her shoulder. It was a graceful exercise and I could see the fire mirrored in its golden blondness, her cheeks glowing, her eyes alive and very dark.

"We have a fireplace in our bedroom," I said, "but we never lay a fire in it. Mary thinks it's messy. It is hard to imagine that woman, Ibsen. It almost seems that she was raised without the pleasure principle. Her whole life is routine. She rises at the same time every day and retires at the same time. You could set your watch by her regularity. When she brushes her teeth (three minutes), when she phones her mother (nine-fifteen) or sits at her Louis Quatorze desk to pay bills (eleven o'clock). It is almost pitiable."

"Perhaps you are more beholden to an orderly life than you realize."

"It is a long road between order and disorder. There are many stops along the trip. Abandon, impetuosity, frivolity. I don't like disorder per se. I like a neat drafting table and a dozen pencils carefully sharpened and sanded in a jar. I don't believe that the dirty grimy atelier is the signature of the true artist. Chagall's studio resembled a surgery, so did Corot's—the colors carefully stored, the brushes well washed and in order."

"Who knows, Peter, I've said this before, perhaps you needed that emotional barrenness to function."

"I don't believe it, Ibsen. I've never felt a greater urge to return to work than this week. I have never been so aware. I've smelled, I have seen textures which have escaped me for years."

Ibsen put down her brush. She shook her head which let her hair settle about her shoulders with measured abandon. I stirred the logs into fresh incandescence. Ibsen watched the fire, she watched me and remained silent.

"You are asking for commitments, Peter. I know."

"I am. Is that so frightening?"

"I think you're feeling I'm quite a gypsy, Peter. I really loved John Perry," Ibsen said. "He had it all, or so I thought. Looks, brains, a sense of humor. I'd been around. Not that promiscuously, really, but there were other involvements, other men I could compare him to. And when it ended, it was very painful. Damned painful."

"His not wanting the child?"

"It wasn't just the child, Peter, although that played a role. I could understand, perhaps, his not wanting a family so quickly. It was . . ."

"What?"

"The brutality of it all. That's what it was—the crassness. I know, I know that we went into the relationship"—she threw up her hands—"what can you call it? Thoroughly modern? An equal footing? I don't owe you; you don't owe me?"

"Like ours?"

Ibsen stared at me, almost not seeing. "Not like ours. Perry kept saying it was supposed to be fun. I knew that. We had the money, and the looks, and the scene was exciting, and we had that wonderful heterosexuality which should be taken advantage of . . . and we did . . .

"No." She shook her head. "There was more. Much more."

It seemed difficult for Ibsen to talk.

"You don't have to tell me all of this."

"Yes I do, Peter. You see, I didn't just lie around the house all day, I didn't just make hors d'oeuvres or chill wines or put out clean guest towels in the bathroom we were to use. Among other things Perry even got another girl pregnant."

"While you were living with him?"

"Yes. 'It was nothing,' he said. She was nothing. In the best Brahmin tradition he was able to write people off as second class, third class."

"Why did he tell you?"

"Because I helped arrange for the abortion. I took the girl to Virginia overnight. Dried the tears, mopped up the blood. There were other sickly situations, his family, his work. I helped. I understood. I *loved* it, goddamn it. Sharing the bitter with the sweet. We were building. I was lover, confidante, accomplice . . . why not? We were getting closer. There was more to the relationship than sex. I was needed. Trusted."

"Well," Ibsen threw a log on the fire, "when *I* got pregnant, I realized how necessary I was. It was my own fault, Peter. He never gave me any reason to doubt that he was a bastard. He spoke about it. His ruthlessness was a trademark. Only I, Ibsen Iazzo, was going to be needed. Crap."

"He's still after you. He's here."

"Sure. He writes. He phones. He's been to Aspen and to Jamaica, now he's here."

"And you won't see him?"

"No."

"Then why don't you tell him to go to hell? Why don't you tell him to leave you alone?"

"I have. I know his game. He once told me about his strategy in diplomacy. 'The art,' he said, 'is to turn defeat into victory, to make fifty-one out of forty-nine, to wear out your opponent with patience.' He's written papers on the subject. I've typed some of them. Besides . . ."

"Yes."

"I'm just enough of a bitch to enjoy his anguish."

The fire was almost out, but the storm was still raging outside. I rose and turned on a small lamp on the desk.

"And our affair is different?" I asked.

"Our affair is different, Peter."

"Why?"

"The roles are reversed. I needed Perry. You need me."

It was a brutal statement and I was not prepared for it. God knows, I had been rejected before. I had been tempered by a hard-willed stern father, honed by an independent wife, but I was not ready to find this sort of cruelty, or even honesty, from Ibsen, my warm, loving, soft, sweet Ibsen, here in the warm winds of the Riviera in this cornucopia of pleasure, of abandon.

"You better get dressed if you're going to that party. It's almost six o'clock, Ibsen."

"What about you?"

"I don't need the Kahn yacht. You do."

"You're not coming?"

"No."

I rose and found my sweater in the bedroom, slipped it over my head, found the little hat I had used on our sail and headed for the front door.

"What about dinner?"

"I think I can manage." I stepped through the door, raced down the steps, and found myself in the rain, half running toward the harbor.

14

I KNEW it would be a mistake to drink heavily this evening, and still I persisted. I found myself in a small quite uncharming restaurant somewhat reminiscent of Sneaky Pete's, and once more I found myself being watched by local fishermen, laborers stopping off for a glass of wine before retiring.

I HAD DATED little during my high school years. I had very little money, my father could not let me use the family car (It's not a toy," he said), I was shy, immature, and it was not until I almost reached graduation that I became friendly with a girl, Ardis Adella, a trim athletic child, as I remember now, with nice tight legs, firm small bosoms, large brown eyes, blond hair clipped short. She played tennis, and played well, beating me regularly with unfeminine abandon. She was neither warm nor witty; she was pretty, and I adored her.

In retrospect, I am sure I frightened her, not because of any great physical advances I made, but because of the very intensity of so many latent emotions, my desire to encompass her life, to tie her down. It was during the full bloom of this romance that Pearl Harbor occurred and overnight I found myself declared an enemy alien. There was no stigma attached to this status except that I was put under curfew, being forbidden to leave the home of my parents after eight in the evening.

At first Ardis complied, seeing me in the afternoons, on Sundays, watching movies, spending hours on the beach, but soon she saw other boys, accepted invitations to parties and dances in the evenings until my anger and jealousy ended the friendship.

We had lived in a one-bedroom apartment at the time and my quarters doubled as the breakfast room during the day. My daybed, curiously vulnerable, seemed halfway in the hall, halfway in the kitchen; I had neither privacy nor freedom and spent most nights under the covers with a small portable radio listening to jazz emanating from distant exotic ballrooms, the Aragon, the Biltmore Bowl, the Waldorf Astoria, but even more painfully I heard the dedications of the disc jockeys: "String of Pearls" to Mike and Mary at the Cove, the Bennie's Boogie to the gang at Hunter's Point, "Moonlight Serenade" to Jimmy and Beanie in Fresno.

Each dedication brought a new image, although all the images were alike, young couples parked in darkness, naked limbs, a hand on a leg, moving up, kisses, warm, wet, long long kisses, hands tousling hair, the smell of gardenias and a touch of Tabu from the mother's dresser.

I had lost track of Ardis, or even people who knew her. Perhaps if I met her I would be able to curse her for all the misery she had caused me, the endless useless times I had thought of her pretty little face, her trim young torso, but even this would be unfair. I had coveted other women, though I had not pursued them, somehow equating marriage with curfew, somehow still feeling like an enemy alien. Of course I had worked this through with Dr. Gerleben, he had surprised me by asking whether I really wanted those affairs or whether I enjoyed the imagined rejection, somehow feeling the need to relive those agonies from adolescence.

But here I was, six thousand miles from home, certainly in ardent pursuit of someone I felt I loved, not fantasizing, not dreaming, but actively doing, taking mature risks, only to find myself again maneuvered into a situation where I could once more imagine Ibsen making love to Perry, once more able to return to the pension, to a dark room, a cold bed and give full vent to my spleen and my jealousies. "A String of Pearls" for Ibsen and John on board the *Valkyrie!*

I had not eaten, watching the food turn cold and gelatinous on the plate in front of me. I had drunk bottle after bottle of vin ordinare set in front of me, and finally rose, paid and was grateful for the moisture in the air when I stood outside. The rain had turned to mist and I half ran, half stumbled to the landing of the *Valkyrie*'s shore boat.

The ship was empty and I waited, the minutes more and more agonizing as I saw the yacht lit and noisy at the mouth of the harbor.

The boy finally arrived, letting several guests out of the speedboat. I gave him fifty francs and pointed to the mother ship and somehow he sensed my urgency and raced across the harbor. It was perhaps eleven o'clock when I stepped aboard the yacht. No one had noticed my arrival, for which I was grateful.

There were several bands in various parts of the yacht, and the combined strains sounded more like a muffled diesel engine, only the various percussion instruments punctuating the silence. I walked about the decks, circumnavigating the yacht several times, fearful of finding Ibsen and Perry sequestered between stanchions and bulkheads. I felt intoxicated, heavy, I did not think what I would say, I could not imagine myself becoming violent. I had plunged aboard the yacht without any control or forethought.

Finding neither of them on deck I started to look through portholes like a thief searching for their faces, knowing they would look in love, bright, cheerful, cool, unconcerned, and did finally manage to spot Perry, dressed as a cowboy, boots, Levi's, a ten-gallon hat on his back supported by a leather strap from his neck. I kept watching him, following him from porthole to porthole, waiting for Ibsen to join him, but finally he stepped on deck and feeling neither foolish nor embarrassed, I accosted him.

"Where is Ibsen?" I asked, simply.

"I really don't know, Mr. Trowbridge. Didn't she come with you?"

176

"I didn't come."

"I see," the young man said, rather charitably.

"I mean I didn't come with Ibsen. You haven't seen her?"

"No. I don't think anyone has. I've asked a number of people whether she was here. Apparently she didn't come."

"Apparently," I said, and nodded, and excused myself, and left, all somewhat simultaneously.

Again I bartered with the dock boy to return me to shore, sitting this time in the bow, watching the Promenade des Anglais approaching, the din from the *Valkyrie* receding, feeling foolish, relieved, perplexed, frightened.

I found Ibsen almost in the same spot where I had left her hours before. She had rekindled the fire and thrown a cardigan about her shoulders.

I took off my sailing hat and stood in front of the fire. My clothes smelled damp, the heat felt good.

"You didn't go to the party," I said.

"No. How did you know?"

"I did."

"Was it fun? Did you find your starlets? Your princesses?"

"I looked for you."

"And Perry."

"And Perry. Perry said you weren't there."

"He was right."

"I made a complete ass of myself."

"That's hard to believe, Peter."

"Well, believe me, I did. Stood there, my eyes red from wine, my breath short from running around that ship, no costume, no necktie, bleating like a goddamned teen-ager."

177

"It doesn't matter."

"What about the Kahn yacht?"

"That doesn't matter either."

"Nothing matters, nothing matters," I shouted, pacing the room, trying to get the wet sweater over my shoulders.

"Is that the way you want to go through the rest of your life? Uninvolved, cool, even-steven, nothing heavy, no hangups, no heavy legs, no double chins? *Something* has to matter, Ibsen."

"*You* matter."

"*I* matter. That's a joke. To whom? The American Institute of Architects? To Mary so I can be a fourth for bridge? To any cock-teaser to get through menopause, to you so you can feel sorry for me?"

"I don't feel sorry for you, Peter. I envy you. I've been sitting here for hours deciding why I am no good to you."

"Why? I love you. I adore you. I want you. Aren't those good valid reasons?"

"I'm really not that wonderful, Peter. It's just that the competition has been poor. If you got a divorce, you'd be the most eligible man in San Francisco. You could have a different Ibsen every night."

"Why are you telling me all this? You were obviously ready to marry John Perry."

"Perry was a different kind of man. He could take care of himself. He's been around."

"I'm forty-two, he's twenty-eight. He's been around. What does that mean? He's slept with more women? He's better in bed? What does it mean, 'he's been around'?"

"The quantity doesn't matter."

178

"What does?"

"He isn't awed because a girl will go to bed with him. You're a fucking pushover with women. Did you know that?"

"The analyst put it differently. It all came to the same thing."

I walked to the bedroom and changed into some dry clothes. I was no longer drunk, really, only tired, confused. I sat on the bed and lit a cigarette, but I could not take my eyes from Ibsen still composed in front of the fireplace.

"What did you have in mind when you suggested I come here with you?"

"A ball."

I nodded my head and rejoined Ibsen in front of the fire.

"Well, it's been that."

"No, damn it, Peter," Ibsen finally exploded, "Why do you believe things like that? I'm a normal healthy girl. I want marriage just as much as any of them. Of course I was excited about you. Peter Trowbridge—Jesus! Why don't you ask some searching questions? Who the hell am I? What's so great about Ibsen Lazzo. A goddamned itinerant set designer. A global gypsy. At least your life has some meaning. You can point to something. Why, why in the hell are we doing all this conjecturing? You want to know about me Peter? You want to know who I am? What I am? I lead a despicable life. Did you know that? Six paper cups, six paper napkins, six paper plates, a bottle of domestic champagne and we'll have a party. And then we throw it all into disposable plastic bags and we dispose of the dishes and the cold hors d'oeuvres and the disposable men and it's another town and another room and another view and another veranda."

"Don't," I said.

"What do you think you'll be getting? All that bullshit. Here, Peter, I want you to see where I live. I want you to see there *is* a home. There is some stability. Do you remember? A year ago in Sausalito?"

"I remember."

"What will you get? The world's second largest collection of cocktail napkins? A closet full of clothes I'm too sentimental to throw out? Three original etchings worth a hundred dollars apiece? Four tintypes of tobacco-chewing forebears in the plains of Iowa?"

"It has a bed with a canopy, Ibsen. A front door that locks."

"It isn't all that simple, Peter."

"I don't expect it to be simple."

I paced the floor, looking at Ibsen, the small fire, the blackness of the night outside the balcony.

"Something happened during the week, Ibsen."

"Something happened," Ibsen repeated, almost to herself.

"Was it Perry's appearance?"

"No."

"Was it?"

"Don't ask any more questions, Peter," Ibsen interrupted.

"You owe me an answer."

"I love you, Peter. I love the way you move and the way you sail a boat, and buy my flowers and tactfully step on the balcony when I undress. I love your goddamned unselfishness in bed. I want to cry about your generosity, oh God,

Peter, don't believe all this woman's liberation crap. That's just for frustrated ladies. I'll tell you what it's like to make love to John Perry. You lie there and provide an opening, moisture, warmth while he masturbates, and his scrotum fills and his penis goes off like a firecracker and then he turns over and winds his Cartier alarm clock. He winds it slowly, carefully to protect the delicate springs while my whole insides are overwound, soiled, abused, emotions in midair like a toy balloon in a breeze, not knowing whether to soar or plunge. Why the hell did you ever waste your time at an analyst?"

"Because nobody ever told me what you just said."

"That's hard to believe."

"I know. Peter Trowbridge. the eternal refugee kid."

"Yeah. Peter Trowbridge, the Village Idiot. Why did you let all those goddamned women kick you around? How much security do you need? You can make it on your own."

"I could if you'd help."

"I don't want to help. You just don't understand, do you, Peter?"

"No, I don't."

Ibsen rolled on her back. She seemed so thin and fragile.

"On the whole," she said, "I like myself. Do you know that? I did until this week anyway."

"You promised nothing. You were honest."

"Bullshit, Peter." She rose and faced me. "I got you to come. I know that. I used all those marvelous feminine tactics. Teasing you, daring you. Christ, I didn't know I'd become such a bitch. I sat here tonight in front of this fire while you were running around town and I really didn't like myself. All of a sudden I could understand your bewilderment when we went to the Kahn yacht. 'Send Ibsen,' that's the war cry. Charming little Ibsen. See Kahn in Nice, see Wertham in Vienna, see Fizother, see Spiegel. You can handle it. That's not why mother spent her hard-earned money to school me. I've listened to that woman. Her eyes are still pretty blue and clear. 'What do you *do*, Ibsen?' she asks. 'What do you really do?' I saw you take my sketches the other day. I knew what you thought. I love you, Peter. Your life makes sense. It makes some kind of sense. Don't ask me to help you screw it up."

"Ibsen."

"No!" She was almost hysterical. "I don't want to go through that divorce with you. I don't want to talk to you about the property settlement or the children or where you'll live or how you'll eat or sleep, damn it anyway, Trowbridge." She threw her arms around me, she was crying, her tears hot on my neck. "Let's go to bed. I want some sleep. I want you to love me. Damn it, Peter. Damn it all."

We made love, but it was cursory, and Ibsen fell asleep, but the events of the week, the day, this evening so occupied me that I found sleep impossible.

I rose and wandered to the balcony, lit a cigarette and stared at the blackness below me. Tightly shuttered, the houses below looked more like stone caskets, the streets empty of traffic and pedestrians only stone streams in a stone forest. A faint moon toyed with the sea, but even the Mediterranean seemed devoid of incadescence tonight.

There was a devastating silence, the mistral had subsided,

I could hear the even youthful breathing of Ibsen asleep in our bed, but strangely each passing minute, each waning hour no longer depressed me. I felt light, almost heady, as if liberated.

I don't want to help you, isn't that what Ibsen said? I don't want to help you, Peter. Can't you see?

And now perhaps I could see. In this strange land on this strange balcony, perhaps for the first time in my life I was becoming an island unto myself. Without Ibsen's help I did not have to be helpless. I *did* have choices. I, Peter Trowbridge, goddamn it, *did* have choices. Perhaps it seems strange to have to wait forty-two years to realize that, and yet, perhaps there were other men who never realized it at all.

I looked at my hands grasping the brass railing of the balcony. They looked pale against the dark metal. I released my hold and rubbed them, putting feeling back into the fingers, and I knew that with these hands I would survive. I knew my trade, I knew that, too, and all these days, these wonderful days my eyes had feasted on the genius of the past, the Renaissance, the Gothic, the baroque, the Norman, the Elizabethan; and I could discern; I could feel a heritage and a challenge. I knew where I could learn, and where I prevailed.

Perhaps it had taken this amalgam of love and beauty, the sacred and profane, the jigsaw of emotions to give me some strength, some confidence. Why question? I knew how I felt and returned to bed. Sleep came more easily than it had the previous nights.

15

WE HAD RISEN at eleven. Ibsen had cooked breakfast with whatever food still remained.

"I call this my Close-Out Omelette," she said, looking fresh and rested from four scant hours sleep, wearing yellow cotton slacks, a lacy white blouse, white sandals, an orange-and-red Dior scarf in her hair, "a breakfast bouillabaisse, a final toast to our delinquent epicurian habits."

"It's marvellous."

"You liar. Here, put some Major Grey's Chutney over it. I find it covers lots of errors."

"I want to go to the Flower Market," I said, "rent a car, take in the Maeght Museum."

"Why all this ambition?"

"Who knows, this may be my last trip to Europe. Fielding says . . ." I smiled.

"What does Fielding say?"

I raised my glass in toast, "To hell with Fielding. Here

184

you peasants," I shouted at Nice below me. "Drink to my love and my fortune."

"Eat your breakfast, Peter. I love you. I want to go back to the *Mistral* before we leave. I want to take another swim."

"I'm eating, darling, I'm eating. We've got a million things to do."

"You're certainly chipper this morning, Peter."

"Why not? Perhaps I learned something yesterday."

Ibsen looked at me somewhat mystified but said nothing.

I helped her with the dishes. We packed our belongings and set the valises near the front door, skipped down the Promenade des Anglais, past Place Massena, and surrounded ourselves with the fragrance and beauty of the Flower Market. I persuaded a marvelously wrinkled peasant woman to fashion a garland of hibiscus and draped it around Ibsen's neck.

It was sunny and warm, the Mediterranean a perfect two-toned blue below us. Bathers in their terrycloth robes left the hotel trying to dodge traffic and photographers to gain the private beaches, the lounges carefully placed on the pebbles like graves in a military cemetery.

I had ordered Campari and soda, my feet were stretched out before me, my clothes getting travel weary, an arm about Ibsen.

"What are you thinking, Peter?"

"I was watching some tourists getting into the cab. They were Germans, did you see them?"

"Yes, but how could you tell they were German?"

"The inevitable raincoat. The Leica. The man inquiring about the fare, then entering the cab ahead of his wife."

"Boor."

"Yes. Probably from my home town." I turned away from the boulevard and looked at Ibsen. She was so beautiful. So very beautiful.

"They're all over the place, the Germans, have you noticed?"

"They bother you, don't they?"

"Yes. They bother me. They have more money than the French, the English. More money than anyone in Europe. Running around guiltless, laughing, loud."

"It has been a long time, darling. That war has been over for twenty-five years."

"Twenty-five years." I nodded. "Six million people. What is twenty-five years? How many of those dead ever saw the Riviera? Ate a pâté?"

"I didn't mean to sound unsympathetic, darling."

"I know."

"Come on, let's get out of here," Ibsen said. "All we do is sit and drink and lie and drink. Let's do some walking, swimming. Come on, you old fart. . . ."

The *Mistral* was not at her mooring and we stood on the dock a little helpless wondering who was on board and where she was headed. We could see the Kahn yacht, imposing and majestic at the opening of the breakwater, a schooner heading into the wind, the crew scrambling on the foredeck to lower the sail. We walked along Rue de l'Opera, Rue St. François de Paule, floating more than walking, holding hands, the boulevards crowded with summer visitors, French, Italians, Danes, English, Americans, all paying homage to Nature and Summer, to the Mediterranean and the sun, the girls in bikinis, and the aproned waiters with brimming glasses of brandy and Pernod. Flags were flying and pennants waved, the stores were open and filled like cornucopias, filled with tourist junk, sweatshirts and phony oils of clowns with tears, Keanes and neo-Keanes, poor imitations of Dufys and Matisses, baubles and bangles, shells and beads, all to end up in a dreary parlor in Cherbourg or Düsseldorf, Toulouse or Milan, Kansas City, Mo., remembrances of a week in lotus land, a week out of context. A candle in a gray corridor. Greetings from Nice, France, a satin-tasseled pillow shouted, and I stopped in the middle of the street and grabbed Ibsen. I kissed her, unaware of the crowds around us.

" 'Greetings from Nice, France,' " I said. She looked at me. "Come on, let's go swimming."

"What about the Musée Maeght?"

"I'd rather look at you in a bikini."

We changed into our suits for the last time at Pension Aida. The bed had been made, the dresser dusted, the mirrors polished. A fresh bouquet stood on the table of the patio, a new package of serviettes awaited the occupants' name. Here one chamber which had held our laughter and our tears was like the *Mistral* ready for new owners, and it made me momentarily sad, as if I wanted to say, no, enshrine it, do not disturb, do not trespass in our world. The chaises had been stacked in the patio, the umbrella folded and encased in plastic, the French frugality punctuating our departure. Even the city below us, lovely and placid almost flouting its permanence against our very transiency, but the gloom did not persist, the sight of Ibsen, her figure lithe and lovely and naked in those two harlequin wisps of cotton made me forget. Nothing is ending, I said to myself, as we skipped to the ocean, nothing is over.

Ibsen crawled long and hard into the gentle surf. I could only see the pink and purple of her fanny as a wave would lift her ahead of me. It was not until she turned on her back to float that I caught her and I, too, turned and stared at the deep deep blue of the sky; the water warm and amniotic beneath me; my toes white and foreign like a procession of ducks, the only point of reference between myself and the horizon. We swam back and lay on the beach.

"Why don't you build us a little house right here? Everyone will come by and say, 'There's a Peter Trowbridge house.'"

"How easy to do a house here. You don't need an architect. Nature does all the work for you. The trick is building quarters amidst congestion. How do you make an island in a jungle? How few of us have worked on that? Just look at that sky. There is sky in Pittsburgh, in New York, there's sky in Hoboken but no, we face everything toward alleys and streetcar sheds. Each man could have a piece of sky. A little shaft of eternity."

"You're always working, Peter, aren't you?"

"Architecture isn't work, my love. What other artist can enshrine his talent in wood and stone and steel and glass?

What other artist can create a work which people use? A place to sleep, to eat, a place to make love and grow old? You *look* at a painting, you *listen* to music, you *taste* a great wine, but you *live* in our work. You *live* in it. What a wonderful, wonderful tribute, what a challenge, what a mission."

"For you, Peter. For you."

"Yes, for me, and for Le Corbusier and for Frank Lloyd Wright and for Sullivan and Mies and to hell with the charlatans.

"Every architect dreams of doing a city. City planners. Big, big projections, parkways, commercial areas, egress, access, site planning, and no one does any work for the little house for the little guy with five screaming kids."

"You're building up a pretty good head of steam, Peter. I think you're ready to go back to work."

"What time is it?"

"I don't know. It must be close to six o'clock. Look at the sun."

"Boy, we better get moving." I stood up and flicked my towel at Ibsen. Once more I looked at her, here on the beach, here in Nice. "Come on!"

We ran to our room, showered, changed.

"Au revoir, Monsieur."

"Au revoir, Madame." There is a finality to a farewell in French. I was happy about the confusion of the arriving cab driver, the bellboy, the concierge, the conversion of traveler's checks, a missing hat box, "Do you have the passports?"

"No, I have them. Au revoir, au revoir."

Neither of us spoke on the drive to the airport and we ignored the driver's attempts at conversation. Once more we traversed the Promenade des Anglais, past the Negresco, the Musée Massena, once more I looked back to catch a glimpse of the port and then the countryside assumed a neutrality, the same neutrality common to every airport, be it Venice or Orly, and I moved the suitcases closer to the door, folded my raincoat one more time, anything to stifle conversation, tears, emotion.

It was a long flight home, the sun keeping pace with the speed of the airplane. I prayed for it to set, but it wouldn't, hovering endlessly above the horizon. We ate lunch and we ate dinner, had apéritifs and wine and cognac, but the monotony of the sky and the light wore us out. We tried to sleep but couldn't manage it, we tried to read but could not concentrate.

It was six in the evening when we arrived in San Francisco, and once through customs I begged Ibsen to put me up for the night. A cab brought us to Sausalito, quite lovely and warm. Ibsen opened the windows of her small apartment, dispelling the fumes of absence. We drank martinis, sitting on her bed, exhausted but too tired for sleep.

We had spoken to each other on our way back from Europe, to be sure, but it was stilted talk, irrelevant. I had not asked searching questions and neither had Ibsen, but I was tiring of this.

"I don't want you to feel guilty about taking me to Europe, Ibsen."

"I don't feel very nice."

"Feel any way you want, darling. You taught me something I should have learned years ago."

"What could I teach you?"

"That I have options."

"You're being very sweet, Peter."

"I'm being very honest."

I watched Ibsen undress, watched as she hung her clothes in her crowded closet, watched as she slipped a flannel nightgown over her young body . . . she fell asleep on my lap.

The alarm woke us at seven the following morning, and Ibsen made breakfast while I showered.

"Where to from here?" I asked.

"Nowhere. I'll phone the studio today. Resign. Perhaps talk to my mother for a while. Tell her I'm going back to architecture. Buildings, homes, things like that."

"Things like that." I smiled and rose, gathered up my raincoat, my suitcase and bent down to kiss Ibsen.

"You wouldn't know a good office that could use a young lady? Bright, pretty, well educated . . . ?"

"I'll ask around."

I found a cab at the corner and gave him my home address. I settled back in the seat of the cab. There was no fog over the city as we crossed the Golden Gate Bridge. I could see sailboats rounding a mark. They would be going windward on their next tack.

005 803 078

Haase   c.1
    Seasons and moments

BROWSING LIBRARY

DETROIT PUBLIC LIBRARY

The number of books that may be
drawn at one time by the card holder
is governed by the reasonable needs of
the reader and the material on hand.
    Books for junior readers are subject
to special rules.